Shorts

Michael Stoneburner

Cover: Else Gilmore

Interior Design: Ryan Coleman

Editor: Jeremy A. Matthews

Printed in Australia

First Printing 2020

ISBN 9780645314205

12ink

Sydney, Australia

michaelstoneburner.com

To all the voices, especially your own.

Table of Contents

I Had One Job

I stood against the wall with my hands deep within my pockets and my eyes slumped. The door to the job agency swung open directly to my left. I had to go inside soon, but I wanted to wait till it was a couple of minutes before my actual appointment. I was either too early or too late. I'd watch other people walk in and they'd say the time that flashed on my phone and would be ushered straight in.

"How do they do it?" I murmured.

The open sign was hung upside down by putty and slid to the floor every few minutes. I tried to fight the urge to fix it myself but I had been pacing outside long enough to know that one of the workers would get up and stick it back up. I wondered if they hated their job or the sign more.

"Perhaps both," I said.

"Excuse me?" a man in a suit paused and looked at me.

I blushed crimson and murmured, "No. Sorry. Not you. I was talking to the sign."

The man gave me a look and nodded slowly before heading inside the job agency.

"I mean," I called out, "I wasn't actually talking to signs! I don't talk to signs I'm not crazy!"

The door closed and the open sign fell. I watched the employer get back up again and push the sign against the glass. I had to wonder if they knew the kind of face they pulled each time they did so.

"Sorry?" a woman asked me as she passed by me on the sidewalk.

"Oh, not you, I was just talking to myself because I'm not crazy. I don't talk to signs."

The woman continued on her way and only looked back at me a few times.

I sighed at myself and thought of the guy who had just entered with the suit. I wasn't wearing a suit. Did I have to wear a suit? This wasn't an actual job interview. This was just the job agency. Surely, I didn't have to wear a suit.

"I should have worn a suit," I grumbled and checked the time on my phone. If I waited just a few more minutes, I could pretend I was one of those people that just walked straight in as if time was mine to bend. I'd just strut right in as if I were wearing a suit.

I adjusted a tie that I wasn't really wearing. I pulled out a comb that I didn't have and brushed hair on the top of my head that I also didn't have. I lifted each of my shoulders up and down and bobbed my head like a rooster. I pretended to take a drag from a cigarette that I'd never have and flicked the imaginary butt onto the ground. I twisted my left foot like Chubby Checkers and grounded the illusory cigarette into the sidewalk and took a step towards the door.

The employer, who kept putting up the sign, stared at me with wide eyes as she stood frozen holding the open sign up against the glass. My body tensed and I quickly spun to my left and kept walking till I was safely in front of the window of the business next door.

I leaned back against the window and sighed, running my hands over my sweaty forehead, "No of course I'm not crazy. I'm just talking to signs, wearing imaginary suits and pretending to smoke a cigarette. Not crazy at all."

I wiggled back and forth as my nerves took over and looked behind me through the window. There was a row of chairs right behind me and two men were turned around looking directly at my ass as it wiggled back and forth. Their eyeline was level to my hips. I pushed myself away from the window and stumbled away. The sweat was getting thicker and I wondered what colour my face had become beyond crimson. I looked back at them in horror and gave a little wave, but their attention turned back to a little boy in red shorts running wildly through the shop.

I looked at the time and swore. Now I was a couple of minutes late. I struggled to get myself to the door and I opened it. The open sign slid down and I struggled to get through the door, pick up the sign and get out of the way of the person who suddenly appeared to enter in after me.

"Well," I joked, "Better take multitasking off of my resume."

No one laughed. The front desk had the same employer who kept putting up the sign. She was looking at me with her wide eyes again and I just slid the sign onto the desk and said, "I'm here for my appointment. Sorry I'm late. I was just...well, there was this guy with a suit and I said I was talking to the sign, but I wasn't…well, I mean I was but not in a crazy way. Is there a way to talk to a sign without looking crazy?"

I snapped my mouth closed to allow her to speak. If I didn't, her eyes looked like they were ready to spill out of her.

"Have a seat," she said as she adjusted either her bra or blouse or both.

"That's a lovely top," I said quickly trying to make up for the nonsense I spewed out before. I watched as her hands stopped adjusting her clothing and covered her cleavage. I gasped in horror at what she must be thinking and forced my eyes to meet hers. "I wasn't….no, see, I wasn't checking out your breasts. I would never…"

"Sit down, please," she sighed as she stood up, grabbed the open sign and went to put it back up onto the glass.

I saw down in defeat and thought of ways that I could show her that I wasn't like that. I was just so nervous. My mind just kept bouncing from getting there too early or too late and not wearing a suit and whether people thought I was crazy or not or if the people in the shop next door thought I was shaking my ass in their faces or if the receptionist thought I was pervert…or worse…I wouldn't be able to find a job. I wouldn't be able to survive for much longer and one chapter of my life had ended and now a new one was beginning. I felt like it was taking an eternity to figure out who I even was or was meant to be…

The man in the suit approached me and said my name and I hissed, "Damn it."

He showed me to a small desk crammed into a corner of

the same room. He eyed me as I sat down and my mouth immediately threw out, "I wasn't sure if I had to wear a suit and that sign must really be annoying. I don't really talk to signs. I'm not crazy. Please find me a job."

He raised an eyebrow and laughed to himself. A few other desks were nearby and in the middle of their discussions until I approached. I suddenly felt their eyes on me as well.

I laughed nervously, "These interviews are never private, aye? We're so close together. Hi, how are you? I see you're all wearing suits. Well, not you ma'am, I'm not saying your clothes look like man's clothes. I'm not saying suits are men's clothes. Women can wear them, too, I'm just saying they're not for me…"

The man in the suit said my name loudly and offered me a seat. I took it too quickly and slammed it into the wall behind it as I plopped down.
"Let's get started, shall we?"

I nodded quietly as the room seemed to settle and return to its cycle. I wondered if they got tired of asking the same questions to different people or if the variety of answers kept them entertained. I then wondered what the odds were that my answers would match exactly to someone else's.

It was then I heard my name a few times and the room's order fell silent again. I blinked my eyes and smiled over at him, "Yes, sorry. I'm just nervous."

"Don't be nervous. We're just going to ask a few standard questions and look over your resume…"

I wondered what my next job would look like. Would I

have a small desk, too? Would I have to do the same thing every single day? What if I had my own sign that kept falling down over and over again? I hated enclosed spaces. I'd get bored with the same questions every day and I'd probably come up with my own questions like, "Do you like goulash?"

"Sorry, what?"

I blinked my eyes rapidly again, "What?"

The man eyed me again and his eyebrows did that thing again where it arched and twitched. I stared at his eyebrow. It had speckles of blonde in it and it looked to be trimmed. They were definitely shaped and I wondered whether he did them himself or got them done. The need to ask him rose in my throat and I willed myself to look at his lips instead. If I stared at his lips long enough, surely, I'd start to actually listen to these pointless questions. He was just jumping through these hoops to get his job done. I'd rather put up a sign over and over again because as least that would be challenging.

"So that's why she does it," I muttered and the man across from me fell silent.

My mouth twitched as he took in a big sigh and asked his question again, "What would you say is your strongest attributes?"

I giggled. The answer sat in my throat but the threat of laughter covered it. I tried to let out a small laugh so that I could speak, but the laugh continued for longer that it should. The man's eyebrow did that thing again and it sent me spiralling. I let out a loud laugh, "Bahaha!"

The sign in the front fell again and I held my sides as they started to hurt as the tears joined in with the laughter.

"I'm not sure I know what's so funny," the man said.

I struggled to form the word. I leaned over and put my hands on his desk. I willed the laughter to fall into the pit of my stomach and avoided staring at his twitching arched eyebrow, "Multitasking."

Montley and Mr. Benedict

"It's odd, you know," he said casually, "living next to the Benedicts. They're so organised, in control, and on top of things. Anyone could watch them, as I do, and know their schedule down to the second."

He scraped his nose against the blinds and continued, "Except for today, mind you. He's left his garage door open again. He is obsessed with closing that thing. Obsessed. Every time I'm out mowing my lawn and he opens that thing he makes sure that thing is closed quick smart. But, not today, or yesterday, or the day before. Why has he forgotten? Perhaps his mind is on other things. I mean, you know how his wife is, so demanding."

He pushed his nose through the blinds and peered through, "I tried talking to her the other day. She stepped through the front door carrying her suitcase. I casually commented on the fact that she had a perfectly good car in the garage, that I could see perfectly because her husband didn't close the garage for days now. I said that she could just place the suitcase in the backseat without struggling to pull the thing to the road. With her nose in the air, I realised that perhaps she was finally leaving Mr. Benedict. I tried to ask her, but you know her better than I do in trying to pry out a conversation with the woman. Heaven forbid I try and be supportive. I know the hours he puts into his work. If he spent as much time with his wife, perhaps she wouldn't be so ridged."

He whipped his head back and laughed, "Montley, you devil you. Oh, dear, I'm going to hell for that one."

He placed his nose back into the blinds, "I never thought the Benedict's garage would be so empty. I was on the phone with Mr. Huntly the other day speaking about this very same thing. For a man who shops all the time at Huntly's Hardware, you'd think his garage would be full of tools. He spends more money in that shop than he does Pott's Flowers. Ms. Pott completely agrees with me when I say that flowers are a quick way to defrost a soul. We do know how cold Mrs. Benedict's soul is. When was the last time we saw her at church?"

Montley's fingers pried open the blinds and covered his mouth. He turned around and squinted through the darkness of the room, "What do you think is happening? I know what I think…"

He laughed forcefully, "Mrs. Benedict is gone. She left that man to be a tart. We can say what we really think. God won't punish us for what we say to someone who can't hear. After all, isn't that what prayer is for? I wish I had tried to get to know her better."

"But quite frankly with the number of times she completely snubbed me, I know exactly what she'd say," Montley stuck his nose up in the air and made his voice squeak, "Please, Montley, I have no time for tea. I am too busy dusting off my husband's tools."

He giggled madly, "Listen to me. I'm the devil today, dear, the devil! I wonder what she packed in that suitcase of hers? Perhaps she packed away all his tools from the garage. This would explain why it's empty. Why do you think it's so empty? Where would he put all those tools? Mr. Huntly still has his receipts. He buys the weirdest tools that only professionals would use. I can only imagine what he does with them. I don't hear any tools being used. Do you? I so wish Mrs. Benedict has been more forthright in her reason for carrying that suitcase out. I would not daresay a word to Mr. Benedict about it. I mean, I hardly talk to anyone at all these days. You know how busy I've been."

He jammed his nose into the blinds again, "I bet she packed away her bloomers. You know the ones, right? Remember the windy day? Those yellow monstrosities flew over to our yard. She was screaming hysterically. For the love of God, dear, they were only bloomers. Bloomers, dear, bloomers!! Crudest things I had ever seen. I was on my way to get the mail, remember? Those things zipped over as if they were trying to escape. They lingered over that road as if wishing the Anderson's kid would come driving through to end its miserable existence. That was the same day Mr. Benedict accused me of checking the mail too often and tried to explain to me that it was only delivered once a day. He obviously hasn't had packages delivered to his house. They have no children, so they wouldn't expect such things. He shouldn't be logging the times when I check the mail anyway. He is by far the nosiest person I have ever met."

The blinds snapped as he pulled his nose back out, "You've seen how he lingers in his yard when he comes home from work. He just stands there staring at his house. Disgusting, really. If I worked the hours he worked, I'd be rushing to get into the shower and wash the filth away. If I washed as often as Mr. Benedict did, I would not ever be bidden in the pearly gates, dear! He's bad news. Mrs. Benedict was right to leave him. I always thought he was bad luck. Do you know how often I bite my tongue when I speak of him? It's a warning from God, you know. It's as if I'm speaking the devil's name. Mr. Benedict. I mean, the devil's tongue is in his name, dear. I am just saying."

Montley stood there in silence for a moment before he raised a finger into the air, "Just the other day, I nicked my chin shaving. Nicked it! I could have bled to death, and it's because of Mr. Benedict. He was doing something loud in his front lawn. I stood on the bathtub to peer out the window to see the commotion and slipped. It was the moment I saw him. He was doing something with Mr. Ednus. Seriously, what would he want with Old Saint? Mr. Ednus was probably trying to beg Mr. Benedict back to church, but they were sharing a laugh. A laugh!"

His fingers pushed aside a few of the blinds, "We were always sensible neighbours. Looking through their windows to see if anyone was home. Short tempered. Both of them. If they didn't want anyone to look through their windows, then perhaps they should keep their curtains closed. Like now. Look at how tightly they are closed. I've never seen them closed this long. I bet it was Mrs. Benedict that opened them daily. He's going to seclude himself now, I bet you. Serves him right, letting a perfectly good woman just walk out his door. She was so lovely. We should have had her over more. But now, look at those windows. Closed tight. Inhospitable. How is anyone supposed to know when they're home or not? Remember the last time I went over to check in on them. The noises I was hearing from within that house was ungodly. Remember? I could have sworn I saw Mr. Benedict give me a crude gesture. But look now, he's alone. No wife. No child. I wonder if he's even showing up to work at all?"

He leaned back and looked up at the clock on the wall, "The car does come and go sometimes. But Mr. Benedict certainly doesn't take note of the time! Just the other night, he didn't get home till eleven! Eleven! That's a good 4 hours passed his normal working time. Can you believe the nerve of him to drive down this street at this hour? He's not quiet about it. Opens that crude garage door, well, not lately, but when he does, I can barely sleep a wink. By the time he gets inside, my whole body aches just standing at the window watching. If I hadn't been reminded by the police as to how busy they are, I would have called them straight up."

Montley took a gulp of air and fell back into his recliner. He stared at the blinds that blocked his view from the Benedict's house and sighed, "It's safest this way, you know, having the blinds the way we do. Just last week, and I don't hold it against anyone in this house, the blinds were left open. Dangerous these days. With Mrs. Benedict gone and Mr. Benedict half-cocked. Did you see the suitcase she took with her? Mrs. Benedict leaving with that god-awful green suitcase. Green suitcases and yellow bloomers! That woman has no sense and yet thinks she has impeccable taste. The arrogance of that woman. I'm quite glad she's gone. I bet she drove Mr. Benedict crazy with her eye for such things."

The house grew silent before Montley started up again, "Oh how she was so organised, though. Poor woman. How did she manage? Mr. Benedict's schedule seems so completely impulsive. I can't stand it. I was saying the other day that that woman was rightly good for him. Who was I saying that to? Mr. Ednus, I think. I bet she went to her sisters. When was the last time she came to tea? I bet she's at her sisters. I said that to Mr. Ednus, as well, and being the Christian man that he is, he was privileged to hear what I had to say. Old Saint is such a good man. He keeps to himself most times, but when he does converse, he listens well. Doesn't say much at all, dear, much at all. It isn't good for the soul to be alone."

He stood back up and lifted the blinds with his chin, "I think Mr. Benedict has completely lost his mind. Hear me? He's completely lost it. That garage has been up all day. Anyone could walk up and open the door into his house, and it's unlocked! Completely mad! I swear if I were his boss, I'd fire him for his hours or lack thereof. He's completely unreliable. I daresay, something is not right here."

Montley buried his nose into the blinds, "Just the other day he came home early. The man can't make up his mind whether he's early or late. He opened his front door. He didn't even put his car in the garage. The car was crooked in the driveway. What's the point of having a driveway if you're only going to park crooked? What's next? Lawn parking?! One of these days, dear, he'll snap. I'm telling you, he will completely snap. I am almost in my right mind to walk over there and have a talk to him. He'll turn to recluse like Mr. Ednus but without God. What would I even say to Mr. Benedict?"

Montley turned away from the window. "I know what I would say. I'd say, 'Oh, hello Mr. Benedict, I am so lucky I caught you home this evening. It's Montley Dupoint from across the street. We haven't talked in ages.' At this point he'd try to close the door on me, but why do you think I wear my boots over? Keeps the door from closing, dear, that's call resourcefulness. So, I'd stand there with my boot in the door and I'd continue to say, 'I was just wondering if Mrs. Benedict will be joining us for afternoon tea tomorrow.' He'd probably tell me she wasn't there but that wouldn't stop me. I'd just say, 'What? She's left? For how long?' He'd tell me, of course. I'm naturally charismatic. 'Oh, how disappointing for us. How are you coping?' No, no, I won't say that. Let's face it. That man is nothing close to incorrigible.

Montley fell into his recliner and sighed, "Mr. Benedict exhausts me."

The Princess of Delovia

Chapter One

Once Upon a Time

Casey was a prince, so his parents told him. His parents were the rulers of Delovia. It was the largest kingdom in all the land and everyone loved them. Everyone that is except Bitemark, a ferocious dragon that lived in a cave high above the clouds. Casey loved to talk about Bitemark because it was the only thing that made everyone uncomfortable. The only thing that is except for when Casey talked about wanting to be a princess.

Casey grew up being told about how great it was that he was a prince and that one day he would be a glorious king. But that didn't make Casey as happy as everyone wanted him to be about it. In fact, Casey was miserable.

He was always asked, "What are you doing?"

Followed by a rather bold statement, "A prince does not do that."

And this is where Casey's story begins, in the Queen's wardrobe trying on a dress she once wore when she was a princess and his caretaker Lord Easton opening the door and asking...again...

"What are you doing?"

Casey looked up at Lord Easton still quite impressed with himself that he was able to squeeze into his mother's dress while standing squished in a wardrobe. His long blonde hair covered half his face and hovered just above his shoulders. He had a slender frame his mother always complained about. He was always told to eat and train more. His mother never believed him when he said that he already did. His body just chose to be slender and petite.

"Hello, Lord Easton," Casey said, automatically beginning to pull the dress off of him. He was having more trouble doing so than he was pulling it on.

Lord Easton let out a loud exacerbated sigh and began, "Prince Delovia,"

Casey mouthed the words as Lord Easton said them, "A prince does not do that."

Lord Easton assisted Casey out of the wardrobe and then out of the dress, "Prince Delovia, why must you do this to your mother? You know she has a terrible fright when she hears about your antics!"

Casey stayed silent as Lord Easton continued to lecture him, "You are young. Naive. But don't let that turn you into a fool. All of Delovia looks to you. You set an example. Such attire is meant for a lady. It shows a level of demeanour that is not suitable for someone in your stature."

Lord Easton always used big words and hear himself talk. He prattled on as they both ensured Casey had on his shirt and vest. Lord Easton was horrified at the sight of Casey's wrinkled pants but they both snapped them up quickly and slipped on his polished shoes.

Casey stood ridged as Lord Easton pushed him out of his mother's room and out into the hallway. A few of the guards dared to give sideways glances and Casey was pretty sure they were the ones who sent for Lord Easton. Casey held his nose in the air as he passed them.

"There is a delegation from Rockford coming today. You are to greet them, Prince Delovia. Your father has requested it and we might be late if we do not hurry along and change your clothes. I suggest the gray suit."

Casey groaned, "With the strangling tie? Why can't I just wear whatever?"

"Wear whatever, young sir?" Lord Easton paused and gazed down at Casey over his rather large nose. Casey refused to look up because he'd just end up counting Lord Easton's white nose hairs. "Let me guess. You'd rather wear the pink dress with the white laces that button up at the nape?"

"Ew, no, Lord Easton, don't be absurd."

Lord Easton nodded, pleased with himself and continued along the hallways before freezing in his tracks when Casey called out, "The red one with the blue satin sash. Isn't that Rockford colours, Lord Easton?"

The hallway was silent until an elegant side door opened and one of the servant girls walked out before reversing quickly at the sight of them and closing the door. Even she could tell that Casey had put Lord Easton in one of his moods.

Casey grinned. He was probably the only one who found Lord Easton's moods extremely funny.

Lord Easton's moods started when he was flabbergasted.

His lips would tremble and he'd slap them together to make words but instead warbling sounds came out instead.

Casey refused to hide his grin but he stifled his laughter at Lord Easton turned around. His lips flapped together. The man kept tugging at his black velvet vest until his chained stop watch jumped out of his vest's pocket and dangled back and forth as if to hypnotise the prince.

Casey found it harder not to laugh the moment the eyes began to bug out of Lord Easton's head and the white moustache bristled back and forth causing the rest of it to tug slightly as his facial hair continued around his mouth and up his chin line.

"Prince Delovia," Lord Easton managed to say, "What would your father say?"

Casey's smirk disappeared.

Lord Easton found more of his voice as he took another step towards the young prince, "You know the cough plagues him. If it doesn't get better, I do not want to imagine what will happen. But if it were to happen, what then? You a king? You can't even get ready for a delegation properly? Must I go to him now, while the cough steals him of his voice and tell him of another one of your transgressions? Must I, Prince Delovia?"

Casey felt guilt spread across his face. He did worry about his father's cough. It had been months now since it forced him to retire to the bed. Rumours were starting to spread that this cough was a curse brought on by Bitemark, the loathsome dragon above the clouds. The cough only came after the last time the dragon attacked the kingdom with his icy breath.

"I shall ready for the delegation at once," Casey suddenly stated and clicked his feet together and marched away from a rather proud Lord Easton. Casey waited till he had rounded the hallway before relaxing his shoulders and exhaling.

He stopped at one of his favourite paintings. It was of his grandmother, Her Majesty Marigold. She was elegant and beautiful and oh could she dance magnificently. Casey's mother always tried to have her dresses made in the quality that was befitting of Her Majesty Marigold, but Queen Delovia was never satisfied with the results.

Casey dared to twirl in the hallway. He clasped his hands over his chest and sighed, "Oh, if only I could be a princess someday..."

28

Hidden Hills

She chased after him down the hallways. His giggled echoed in the emptiness of night. He was supposed to be in bed hours ago, but she had lost herself in her painting and he had lost himself in his toys spread across the living room floor.

"You little bugger," she playfully grumbled as he either dived into his room or his wobbling legs had sent him sprawling forward, "Get yourself into that bed."

His giggles were infectious and she couldn't help but laugh as she slowly stalked down the hallway, "Fee. Fie. Foe. Fum..."

A shrill giggle of expectation came first before she entered his room and he scrambled up off the floor and dived into his bed.

"I'm in bed, mommy," he said, "that means I'm safe."

She pretended to be disappointed and crossed her arms, "I guess so. Lucky. I was really hungry for some tickles."

His eyes widened and his lips mouthed silently, "Oh no."

She stood there for a moment before a corner of her mouth

slowly rose and he gasped and quickly ducked under the covers. She leapt onto the bed and howled, "I want those tickles anyway!"

She laughed while he squealed as she tickled him until he called out, "Okay, I'm tired, mommy!"

She stopped, "You are? Well, we better get you to bed."

She got off the bed and fiddled with the blankets as he snuggled himself underneath them. His round eyes looked up at her and she melted into a smile.

"Bedtime story, mommy?"

She couldn't say no. She wouldn't. Like her paintings, these stories fuelled her imagination and each night as the words drifted out of her lips and into his ears, she could watch his eyes grow heavy until his imagination would take over. She always wondered what he dreamt about.

She climbed into the bed and lay above the covers besides him. She kissed the top of his head, "I love how you love stories. Tomorrow we'll go to the library. Until then, you alright, my love, you ready for bed?"

He nodded and wiggled himself deeper into his pillow and she closed her eyes and like the colours in her palette, her words began to paint his dreams:
"Why can't the sky stay its blue even when the day is through, and why can't the moon keep its light when the stars come out at night?"

"Why, mommy?"

"The answer lie like most answers do, beyond the light and above the blue, where fields of countryside abide, where hills and grass peacefully hide."

He sighed and her eyes opened to check in on him, but his eyes were already closed and she could tell by the look on his face that he was listening and trying to imagine such a place. She smiled a soft smile and brushed his cheek with her lips and continued:

"There rests a back porch where a lullaby sings, a simple song an old woman brings."

She watched as a smile spread across his face and she nodded softly, thanking the old woman silently as she rested her head against his pillow, closed her eyes and continued:

"Every day before the sun slipped down to sleep, white fluffy clouds, blue skies it sweeps.
At her house there is nothing ever wrong, for the sun slept easy thanks to her song.
The sun knew she'd wake again when she heard that old woman's lullaby and rise above the horizon, her rays would happily sigh."

"But, mommy, who is the old woman?" his voice snapped her out of her tale.

She giggled softly, not opening her eyes, "You know who it is, my love."

"Milly?"

"Yep."

He grew quiet so she knew she could continue, "The sun would see Milly sitting in her lovely wooden chair, the soft winds dance throughout her hair. The trees rustled down to join in her nap, the hills lay hidden in shadow's lap."

Her tone began to deepen as she continued, "The grass lay quietly against the ground, while Milly's magical song spread around."

She hummed a bit as he suddenly turned to her in bed and his small arm wrapped around her and squeezed. At first Milly's song began as a whisper until it filled his room:

"Tonight has come and so will Moon; the stars will shine upon the loon.
Shadows make for all the hill's beds and all the flowers close their heads.
So hello, Moon, and goodbye Sun, for this is how the night has begun."

He sighed happily and whispered, "Milly..."

There was a moment's silence where she wondered if Milly's song had already worked and just as she was about to slip out of bed, his voice quietly rose from his lips, "Will the night stay forever, mommy?"

"Oh, no, my love," she whispered and relaxed again. Tonight was a night she'd have to stay to the end. "Milly would never let the darkness stay."

She stroked his back and continued:

"The answers continues like all answers do, beyond the light and above the blue,
where fields of countryside abide, where hills and grass peacefully hide."

He faintly whispered something but she didn't hear it.

Sleep was beginning to take over him. She continued more for herself than him:

"Resting on that porch where a lullaby sings, a simple song Milly always brings.
Every night before the moon slipped down to sleep, twinkling stars, black skies it sweeps.
At Milly's house there is nothing ever wrong, for the moon slept easy thanks to her song.
The moon knew she'd wake again when she heard Milly's lullaby, rise above the horizon, her beams sigh.

"She'd see her sitting in her lovely wooden chair, the cool winds dance throughout her hair.
The trees, holding birds, singing wake, the hills fill with colour, the grass would shake.
Everything would wake on Hidden Hills ground, while Milly's magical song spread around:

"Today has come and so will Sun; the birds will sing for everyone.
Here comes the blue; here comes the green and all the colours the world has seen.
So goodbye, Moon, and hello Sun, for this is how the day has begun.

"So, why can't the sky stay its blue even when the day is through,
and why can't the moon keep its light when the stars come out at night?

"It's because everything needs a rest sometimes, it's allowed, even for the lovely Ms. Milly Cloud."

She slid herself carefully out of his bed and fixed the blankets before kissing him on the forehead and switching off the bedside lamp. The light from the hallway guided her back to the door where she stopped and looked at the picture hanging on the wall beside the door frame.

A young girl was holding a baby wrapped in a blanket. She remembered how frightened she felt holding her son but like the picture showed, an old woman had an arm wrapped around her shoulders. Her eyes twinkled and between two wrinkles, she held a proud smile as they both stood in front of her flower shop.

"Milly," she whispered and touched the photo before disappearing out into the hallway.

And so, this is how the story goes, for how much longer nobody knows,
Milly would step out of her house with song, in Hidden Hills nothing ever went wrong.
She'd wait there on the porch where her lovely wooden chair sat, knowing her daughter and grandson knew where she was at.
She'd sing her song until each one would come, her beloved moon and her gorgeous sun.
And when they both slept the blue would come and so would green and all the colours the world had seen.

The Rock and the Roll

The children settled down around the empty chair as the librarian quieted them. Reading Time was about to begin and the parents had already scattered to do their photocopying, using the internet or scrolling through the books. A feeble man slid onto the chair and the children grinned. The librarian shared their smiled as she returned a book, *Geneva and the Other Daughters*, back to the shelf and left. She knew that they were in safe hands.

The old man rubbed his hands together and snapped a finger, "Hello, boys and girls, you'll never believe what happened to me just the other day. I had just finished my chores when I decided that I deserved to treat myself to a homemade roll. I wanted the tasty homemade roll. One that giggled when you poked it. So soft and fluffy. Does that sound good?"

The children nodded. Some of them whispered, "Yum."

"With butter and jam. Just how I liked it. You might like it with just jam or better with butter, but not me. I loved a fresh roll with melted butter and then just a teaspoon of jam, mixing it all up and squeezing the roll together. It's the best."

All the children had gaping mouths and nodded. Their

stomachs started to rumble.

"But my story isn't about trying to make you hungry. My story is about this homemade roll."
The man leaned on his knees and grinned down at them, "I made the roll so perfect that it giggled before I even touched it. It was as big as a grapefruit!"

The kids listened intently but he paused for a moment before continuing, "No, it was as big as a watermelon!"

The kids' eyes widened and their mouths went, "Wow."

The man's eyes twinkled at this reaction and continued, "And the smell, boys and girls, the smell, it made my mouth water. I had put butter on it as it baked and the melting butter just drooled over the sides. I think my mouth was watering butter it was so good. It was the most beautiful roll I had ever made."

"Did you eat it?" a little boy called out. His mother was close by reading a book about painting and closed it for a moment, "Shhh."

"That's alright," the old man winked at her and answered the boy's question, "I couldn't eat it. It was too hot! So, I opened up the blinds to my window and set it on the sill like my mother had taught me to do. I had to wait till it cooled down so that I could eat it."

"What did you do then?" another child called out.

"Well," he said, "to be honest, I decided to go shave. I noticed my face was getting scratchy. But I said to that roll, I said, 'I'll be back with a smooth face so that I can eat you.' I wiggled away with excitement. I couldn't stop licking my lips. But, boys and girls, guess what?"

"What?" they exclaimed.

"I don't think that roll liked that idea at all! In fact, I think that roll thought she was too gorgeous to be chewed up by my teeth. She wanted to live long and beautifully. So, you know what I think that roll did?"

"What?!" they exclaimed louder.

"I think that roll called out to the wind and said, 'Oh, Wind! Wind!'"

The children laughed at the high-pitched voice he put on for the roll.

"What's so funny? Didn't you know that's what rolls sound like when they talk?"

They all laughed and a few of them said, "Noooo. That's silly."

He repeated in his high-pitched voice, "'Oh, Wind! Wind!' I mean, it's a lovely voice, don't you think?"

"Nooooo," the children laughed, "It's funny!"

"How rude," the man joked and continued, "I think that roll begged the wind to blow her far away from that opened window so that I couldn't eat her. 'Blow me far away from this ugly man!'"

The children fell into hysterics.

"'If you take me far away, I will reward you with my mouth-watering aroma!'"

The man changed his voice to a very deep voice, "'You do

smell delicious,'" before changing to his normal voice, "the wind said to the roll."

Some of the children had tears from their laughter. The man took a moment to stay quiet. He looked up to find a lot of the adults engrossed in the story as well. Some others didn't look too pleased with the noise.

A little bit quieter and still in the deep voice, he continued, "'I will smell so good! I will help you, roll.'"

The children quietened, too, so they could hear the rest of the story.

"The wind swept up my homemade roll and took away her delicious smell. She fell from the window and into the mud as the wind ran away with her aroma. She pouted at her misfortune. 'How unlucky for me,'" he said in his high-pitched voice pouting with a big bottom lip. "She had gotten away from the hungry man but now she was stuck in the mud. Her soft and tender self did not have the strength to get out of this dirty situation!"

"'Oh, Rock! Oh, Rock!'" he cried in his high-pitched voice, making kissing faces with his lips.

The children rolled around in hysterics again.

He waited for them to calm a moment before going, "I just don't see what's so funny. She has a very lovely voice!"

"Oh, Rock!" he did the voice again and grinned at the reactions of the kids, "'Move me far away from this dirty mud. If you do, I will reward you with my soft and tender self! Please!' The rock was very cranky for being woke up and grumbled, 'What? What what? What is this? To be soft and tender? Like a pillow? Oh, I'd sleep better like that!' So, the rock moved the roll out of the mud. Her soft and tender self was taken from her. Within moments, the rock was snoring so loudly."

He began to snore and pretend to fall asleep at the chair.

"Wake up! Wake up!" the children cried. "What happened to the roll?"

He pretended to wake up and cried, "Oh, sorry, did I fall asleep? Yes, yes, the roll. What happened to the roll as she rolled down the street? Well that poor roll realised that she was no longer the mouth-watering, sweet and tender roll that the ugly man had once loved. She was no better than what the rock had been! And that mud had made her stink!"

"Ewwww!" the children cried.

"Mr. Dupoint," a little girl said, "this story is making me sad."

He leaned over, "How do you think the roll felt? She was as hard a rock. She smelt like mud and let's face it, I was not going to eat that roll. She felt like nobody loved her at all."

The children grew quiet. Sad looks spread across their faces.

"The rock woke up, though and heard her lovely voice," he winked to some of the parents, "The rock's heart was now soft and tender. He rolled after her and helped clean her up. He took pity on her and gave back her soft and tender self."

Some of the children smiled.

He continued, "And the wind? Well, boys and girls, the wind had been watching the whole time. Saw what the rock did and took pity on her too. The wind picked her up and swept her back to my window sill and gave her back her aroma. The roll was back to her good ole self and she said in her lovely voice, 'I'm me again!'"

"Yay!" the children squealed and clapped.

"'Oh, Rock! Oh, Wind!' she cried, noting her own lovely voice," the adults listening and the children all laughed and disagreed as he continued, "'Thank you. I shall be loved for my beauty and my smell. And especially my voice!'"

The children both clapped, laughed and said, "Noooo, not the voice!"

"But you know what," he said with a glint in his eye, "she was loved for her beauty and her smell. For when I came back, I loved her smell and the sight of her so much that when I returned from shaving, I ate her right up."

The children gasped and many of the parents laughed.

"But, boys and girls, you need to understand, with beauty there comes a price," he stood up and bowed as the library clapped for him, "Now how about I read you some books?"

Cream

I didn't think it was ever possible to be fired from a job agency before until I got a phone call from the district manager saying that they would be transferring me to another office.

"So," I laughed nervously, "that office is technically firing me?"

I made jokes to lighten situations. That's probably why I didn't get a lot of second interviews. Nothing breaks my nerves down more than by making someone smile and laugh. When no one smiles or laughs, I wonder if it's because I needed a better joke. So, I up my game. But then there are situations where my jokes are just not appropriate with the circumstances I was in.

Like now.

"Mr…"

For example, right there, in her tone I could hear that she was being serious. She was not amused by my jokes and later on when I'm rational and calm, I'd look back at this conversation and think to myself that normal people would pick up on that and consider taking it seriously.

I, however, did not.

"…I just feel," she had been talking the whole time and I stopped listening. I was too busy keeping myself calm. I was thinking of the next punch line I could say that would make her giggle a bit and everything would be okay, "that this office is not a good match for you."

"It's because I kept picking up the sign, isn't it? I saw the sign, you know? I opened up my eyes and saw the sign. Shooby doo wop." I winced. Did I seriously do the doo wop?

"Excuse me? Shooby do what?" she asked.

Strike two. She didn't get the reference. This wasn't going well.

"Your next appointment is on High Street next Tuesday at 9am," she just continued painfully through the conversation. Even I recognised that she just wanted the phone call to end.

I pretended to adjust a tie even though I wasn't wearing one, "I feel like I'm going for an interview at a job agency. The irony."

I could hear her roll her eyes at me as she hung up.

I slid my phone in my right pocket and patted my wallet and stared at the café across from me. It was just a smaller one situated in the shopping centre between the cinema and the shopping centre. I went to step towards the café thinking nothing but a double mocha chocolate chip Frappuccino bought vicariously from a credit card I had no business using because I was pretty sure that I was close to maxing it out again when I almost ploughed into a person playing with their headphones hanging around their neck.

I took a deep breath as if my mental rambling were actually said aloud, "Sorry." I called out to the headphone user but they didn't hear me. "Wow, you might as well be wearing your headphones. Okay, time to chill out."

I walked up to the café and joined the line, muttering to myself, "So I got fired from a job agency and have to go to another. Better than having a panic attack and resting against a window unknowingly and plastering your padded butt cheeks against the glass…"

"Sir?"

I looked up. I had absentmindedly followed the line all the way to the register. The barista looked at me with an eyebrow raised. I blushed, "Sorry, yes, yes. What do I want?"

I stood there for a moment. My mind was racing. Was I talking out loud? I think I was. Which means she had heard everything. How long had I been standing there for?

"I'll have a double mocha chocolate chip Frappuccino, please and my butt isn't padded. I was just being dramatic."

The woman's eyebrow arched higher and I imagined it crawling straight up her forehead and diving off the top of her head saying, "Yep. I'm out."

I just needed to sit down. I needed a breather. I needed to catch my breath from the disaster that was the day and lose myself in chocolatey goodness. Was that too much to ask?

"And would you like cream on top, sir?"

"Yeah, just cream me all over," I quickly said and suddenly forgot how to breath. My eyes widened and before I could stop my flustered lips I quickly continued, "I mean, the Frappuccino. Not me. I wasn't being inappropriate. Just excited about the drink. But not THAT excited! Like I wasn't talking about you..."

My voice faltered. My lips wobbled. My brain was screaming at me not to whisper it, but I did, "...you know, sperm."

You'd think I'd stop there.

"I mean, you're a girl, you can't even..."

"SIR," she said loudly and quickly, "it's $7.99. Cash or card?"

I wanted to thank her for stopping me. My mouth slammed shut. My face was red and sweating. I pulled out a card and nodded, "This is probably why I was fired from a job agency."

Spy Train

Clickety-clack. Clickety-clack. Clickety-clack.

I gave a grave smile and went to sit down. A little jerk from the train sent my butt smacking down harder than expected onto the seat. My cheeks burned with embarrassment. This always happened to me. As carefully as I try to do anything, I somehow find a way to draw attention to myself. I had walked slowly down the aisle. I had scoped out a designated seat that gave me plenty of room. I avoided eye contact and physical contact and still, I found a way to get attention.

The seats were empty around me. I hoped it would last, and as the train continued to pick up speed, I was confident that this train ride would be a comfortable one. That was, until someone sat across from me. I couldn't see passed their newspaper, even as they sat down. Who read their newspaper while they walked through a train?

No one else was around. I was alone with the person reading the newspaper.

I wonder what he looks like, I asked myself.

The newspaper rustled as the person turned to the next page. My eyes travelled down to the person's clothing, well, the parts that I could see anyway.

He's a he. I bet myself, but not wanting to judge the person unfairly I made sure to look at all the clues. He wore thin, blue pants that were neatly ironed and black shiny shoes. Each shoe had an equal length of lace. I could tell because I was mentally measuring it.

He's totally in business. An associate of something, I'm sure. I nodded my head, agreeing with this thought. I stared at the man's brown leather gloves that held the newspaper.

Wait a minute. It isn't cold outside. What's up with the gloves? He must be hiding something. Perhaps he has some sort of horrible scarring on his hands. I bet he was in some sort of fire. Perhaps he stumbled upon some files while doing business. They tried to shut him up and...

I covered my mouth. Maybe he stumbled upon a plan to smuggle drugs into the country.

My heart began to beat faster. I shifted in my seat uncomfortably. I was sitting across from some sort of spy.

Oh my God, I thought, almost falling off of the seat. He's wearing gloves because he killed someone and the police are trying to find a suspect in the murder case but he did such a good job covering up his fingerprints that it will soon be dropped! Unsolved!

My face paled. I had been so careful. I had chosen an empty part of the train. Why did drama always find me?

I looked down at my trembling hands. A great dread made it hard for me to swallow. I began to pray that I would not be dragged into the man's evil plot. I scooted more towards the aisle so I had a clear runway just in case the spy tried to attack me.

Look at him. He's just sitting there reading the newspaper probably so smug, so proud that he got away with it. I bet he's trying to find an article about the assassination.

I choked on my own spit.

That's what it is. He assassinated some sort of politician because they threatened to close down his drug smuggling business. He couldn't have it shut down, so he killed the politician. But who? Which one?

Sweat dripped down my forehead.

I've got to stop this man before he kills someone else! What if it's a prime minister or a president or the queen? The queen?! God save the queen!

My heart almost stopped. I felt sick to my stomach. Suddenly, I wanted to get off the train.

My thoughts screamed at me and bubbled out of my mouth as a squeak. I slapped my hand across my lips and stared at the newspaper.

They all probably know about this guy. They are probably searching desperately for him. I could be the only one who could stop him!

I imagined what they'd say to me after I thwarted the evil spy, Earth owes a huge debt of gratitude to one man who fought the good fight. He stood up against the world's most deadliest spy, and if it weren't for his bravery, we, the prime minister, the president, and the queen, wouldn't be alive today. So, on behalf of all the citizens of the world, we honour this man with the key to the world.

Hope in my heart brought back my courage, and I looked towards the front page of the newspaper and sneered to myself, You won't get away with this. The lie you call your life will be stopped by none other than me.

I tugged at the collar of my shirt and pounded my chest hard. I winced and rubbed it slightly. The newspaper snapped quite suddenly, sending me almost crawling up onto the seat.

I shivered as doubt replaced the hope I had gathered. One of the gloved hands disappeared behind the newspaper. I hugged my knees to my chin and stared with wide eyes.

He's going to shoot me. Oh my God, he's going to shoot me. He's going to kill me because I know too much. I regret sitting here. I didn't know what I was getting myself into. I didn't know that he had so much guilt on his shoulders. God. This is why I don't sit next to strangers. I hope for friendliness, and this is what it gets me every freaking single time. I sit next to someone on a train, and they pull me into their sick lives.

I had only one wish on my mind now. I wished that I could update my last will and testament so my life would have some sort of closure. I shook my head, fighting off the tears.

I can't worry about this right now. Right now, I need to get out of here without dying.

My head slammed into the back of the seat when the man coughed. Panic was only just now beginning to take over my mind. I bit my bottom lip and continued trembling.

How can I make him believe that I won't tell a soul? I thought to myself.

His gloved hand went behind the newspaper and reappeared, placing a brown paper bag beside him. My eyes stared with suspicion and awe.

He's been hiding that bag behind the newspaper! I screamed to myself, he thinks he has the upper hand now that I'm his hostage. Hostage? Oh my God, mommy, I'm a hostage. Look at him. Sitting there all calm while I'm his hostage. I envy his confidence, but I can't give up now. I bet if I get my hands on that bag, I'll have all the power, and the prime minster, the president, and the queen would be saved!

My eyes travelled to the newspaper while I slowly slid my feet back to the floor. I pretended that I was stretching as I leaned forward and slowly reached for the bag. As my arms slowly dropped, the man moved his right hand down quickly and thrust it inside the bag. The newspaper shifted again and the gloved hands lifted something large and black.
Frozen in place, I peed a little.

It's a gun. It's a gun! That's where he was hiding the gun. Curse you evil spy man!
I cursed myself for my failure and slid back into my seat. My failure had cost me my life.
Will anyone grieve my death? I failed to save the president, the prime minister, and the queen. My family will be disgraced. I live alone. I'm a nobody on a train.

My eyebrows lifted and I dared a smile. Yeah, I'm a nobody. A complete waste of space. Who would believe someone like me? I live alone. My family is disgraced. I have a sorry excuse for a life. No one would believe this story even if I told someone.

My smile spread even wider as the gloved hand placed the large, black object back into the paper bag. I would relive that moment over and over again later when I was safely back home. I silently clapped my hands together and grinned.

The man realised that no one would believe me anyway, so he had no need to kill me. I am a mere simpleton. No one would take me seriously because I'm just a pathetic man who has nothing better to do than make up stories. Wait until people at work hear about this!

I covered my mouth quickly, but it was too late. I had already thought it. The gloved hand once again returned to the bag and pulled out the large, black object. The hand disappeared behind the newspaper again.

I folded my fingers together in prayer and frowned. My bottom lip was trembling.
I'm screwed. No use pleading for my life now. He'll kill me for sure.

Clickety-clack. Clickety-clack. Clickety-clack.

The train hissed to a stop. I sat back in defeat and prepared for my untimely death. The gloved hands folded up the newspaper and lowered it. My jaw dropped in horror as the man's face was revealed to me.

"Oh, excuse me, dear," the old woman smiled shyly, "would you happen to know what stop this is?"

A small squeak spilled out of my open mouth.

I drooled a little.

My eyes travelled to her gloved hands. She giggled and tucked the magnifying glass away into her little brown purse.

"My eyes aren't what they used to be. Don't worry, dear, I'm pretty sure this is my stop."

I squeaked again.

She slowly stood up and headed off the train, leaving me alone once again.

"I can't believe this," I finally spoke, "that was the best disguise I have ever seen!"

The Princess of Delovia

Chapter Two

The Fairest Grandmother

"What are you doing?" a shrill voice echoed the hallway and put Casey's twirling to an end.

His eyes had closed sometime between mid-twirl as he imagined himself in one of his grandmother's gowns dancing around the ballroom in the arms of a knight in shining armour. Casey froze and his eyes snapped open to the scowl of his mother at the doorway to his bedroom. Next to her stood a gaping servant.

Queen Delovia snapped her fingers in front of the servant's face, "Don't just stand there gawking at your prince! Get inside and help him prepare for the delegation at once! And you," she snapped her fingers at Casey next, "what are you doing? There is no time for your silly little games, Casey. You know your duty and must take your place at my side to greet our guests. If your father…"

The servant was slowly easing his way into Casey's room still eying the prince.

"And they are silly little games!" Queen Delovia barked into the ears of the servant as he rushed into Casey's bedroom. She turned back to Casey who approached her sheepishly. "If your father were able, he'd be horrified at your antics. Now get in that room, now. Where's Lord Easton? I swear sometimes he's neglecting his duties with you…"

"I am here," Lord Easton grumbled as he came up behind Casey and bowed, "I had just retrieved Prince Delovia… ahem…from your wardrobe. I was ensuring nothing was amiss. Unless you preferred that I didn't and left him to his…silly little games?"

Queen Delovia grew flustered and pulled out her folded-up fan and flicked it open so she could fan herself, "No, Lord Easton, I appreciate it. The delegation will be here soon and Prince Delovia is far from ready. Please see to him, won't you?"

"Of course," Lord Easton bowed again, "your majesty, as you wish. Shall I fetch the gray suit? I believe that is your favourite."

"No!" snapped Casey at the same time his mother exclaimed, "Yes!"

Queen Delovia snapped her fan closed and returned it to a pocket that had been somehow hidden in one of the flourishes of her dress, "Not another word out of you, Casey. Not today. It is important that this delegation see us as a strong and dependant kingdom. We must not falter with our Lord King in his frailties."

"Just tell them Bitemark…" Casey began but a stern eye from his mother shut him up quickly. "Yes, mother, I shall wear the gray suit."

"Thank you," she sighed, lifted up her dress so that it didn't drag on the floor, turned and walked away with surprisingly grace for someone so flustered. Casey was almost in awe.

"Shall we?" Lord Easton asked, moving over to the bedroom door and motioning a hand to it.

"I shall, Lord Easton, but you shan't," Casey snapped and barged passed him to the door, opened it, stepped inside and turned, "But as your prince I command you to go to the greetings hall and wait for me there. I shall put this horrid gray suit on myself."

"But, sir," Lord Easton began but Casey slammed his door behind him as he walked inside.

The door reopened and a servant was practically flung out and Casey snapped, "And take this thing with you!"

Casey locked the door behind him and slammed back into it. Hot tears streamed down his face and he flung himself across the room and into his bed. He raged cried into his soft blankets and punched at the air. He refused to put on the gray suit.

"I absolutely refuse," he hissed, as he pushed himself off the bed and strode quickly across the room to his fireplace and then back again to his bed. "I would rather go naked than put that ugly, constricting suit on this body!"

His eyes rose to above the mantle place of the hearth and stared at a family portrait that hung carelessly above it. Her Majesty Marigold stood to the left-hand side of the painting. She was wearing a red rose dress with blue satin sashes. His mother had tried to duplicate it but it wasn't as elegant as the one in the painting. Next to Her Majesty Marigold stood the King, Casey's father, dressed in a somewhat gray suit himself looking elegant yes, but Casey sneered at it anyways. His mother stood next to him and standing in the front of them both was a young Casey with a goofy grin and hands behind his back. He remembered standing for that portrait. He was holding onto a makeshift doll he had made from the bedsheets.

"Boys don't play with dolls," Casey mimicked his father's voice on the day as he continued to pace back and forth between the hearth and his bed. Casey kept pacing for a few more times before he looked up at the painting again, "Oh, grandmother, you always asked me whether the dresses were suitable. You told me I had such eyes for things. Well, how can I see with them if people are always trying to blind me?"

Casey continued pacing a few more times muttering to himself. He was trying to convince himself to put the damn suit on. But everything in him told him not to.

"Do not be a deviant," Casey mimicked his father's voice again and added another thing his mother would say, "And especially, Casey, do not be defiant."

"Oh, but darling," a voice snapped Casey out of his revere, "those were your most appealing qualities."

Casey looked around the room. He knew that voice. It was so familiar. A voice he had not heard since he was a boy.

"Poppycock and Fiddly Faddly Fee," the voice echoed throughout his room. "time to open up those eyes and show the world who truly sees!"

Casey's eyes darted up to the portrait and he gasped. Her Majesty Marigold was missing from the painting and the little boy was proudly standing there holding a makeshift doll.

"Bibs and Bobs, ignore those snobs," a voice whispered from behind him, "because my dear Casey, believe it or not, you're not the one full of Fiddly Faddly Fee and Poppycock!"

Casey spun around and squealed. On his bed, resting just where he had laid moments ago and had his fit, was a red dress with a blue satin sash. It sparkled like glass in the light. Casey rushed over to it.

"Well," the voice echoed throughout the room, "what are you waiting for, child? Put it on and snap that delegation to attention!"

The voice faded and as Casey reached for the dress he hesitated. The dress vanished and Casey's heart dropped into his gut. His head dropped in disappointed with eyes closed and tears beginning to come.

"It was all a dream," Casey whispered.

Casey suddenly felt strong elegant hands on his shoulders and a soft whisper tickled his ear, "Open your eyes and see."

Casey's eyes flung open and he gazed down at himself. His body was covered in red, sparkling velvet and around his waist hugged a blue satin sash.

Casey squealed and twirled around the room, "I'm a princess!" He twirled a few more times before rushing to the door and stopping before opening it. His eyes gazed up at the portrait and again he gasped. Her Majesty

Marigold's image had returned; however, she was nude.

"Thank y—ew, grandmother," Casey hissed and quickly left the room. "I said I wanted to see but that's just too much."

Seeking

I stepped into the shopping centre, pulled off my headphones and draped them around my neck. Today was window shopping. It was a term my grandmother always used, especially if I wanted to buy something. She'd just tell me we were only window shopping and wink at me. I was never sure of why she winked. I just thought she was being honest with me, but now I see that perhaps she was telling me something more. I was window shopping because I needed to get out of the house. I hadn't left in days. Just didn't need to, but let's face it, I just didn't want to. I had trouble feeling safe around people. I was also only window shopping because I had no money to spend and with what I know about my family, we didn't have much money. So perhaps telling me we were window shopping and winking was a way to hide their own disappointment.

My eyes explored the people around me. I wasn't living in a small town but the local community was familiar enough. I was waiting to recognise someone, but no one gave me that familiar nod and smile. And if they were extremely chatty, I'd have to say hello and tell them how my mother was doing. It's why I took my headphones off. People weren't afraid to tell you if you were being rude and there were still some shops that insisted you had shirts and shoes because if not, no service.

I had a few shops I'd actually enter but a majority of them

I'd just look, especially if it was a clothing shop. When it came to buying clothes, I already knew what I wanted before leaving the house. I didn't want to spend too much time searching through all these clothes that I'd probably only wear once and then it'd hang in my closet for the rest of its life feeding the moths.

I passed the cinema and looked at the movies. Black Paper was still listed. I wanted to see it on the big screen but the bills were piling up. I'd have to wait like most movies. The rental stores had long since disappeared so online was the only place I could find the ones that I missed. But so many people were saying Black Paper was so good. An intense ride, I once read from an online critic I followed.

I passed a little café that lived vicariously between the cinema and an electronics store. A woman had her child beneath a blanket and I smiled and quickly looked away.

"That reminds me, I need milk," I said aloud and an old woman with a brown purse gave me a look before I shrugged and quickly added, "Sorry, sorry."

The walkway widened and split into four ways to go. I'd come back to the electronics store, but first I wanted to go to my shop. A shop full of games, toys and other memorabilia. I was only going window shopping but I was also panicking hoping they still had items I've wanted for months now.

In the center of the intersection a juice store sat with a line of people ordering their drink. I joined the line and wondered what I would get. Sometimes I'd listen to people in the line. Searching for gossip. Sometimes I'd hear about people I actually knew. It wasn't a big enough town to be able to talk about other people so openly. So, hey, if they were willing to take that chance, I was willing to listen.

It wasn't like I was a busy body. I didn't spread the gossip. I just casually listened intently. Okay, so maybe I was a busy body but I wasn't malicious about it.

"You hear about Mr. Stone?"

"The author of Amulet of Fire?"

"Local legend, aye?"

"Yeah. You read his books?"

"Nah, did you?"

"No."

I rolled my eyes. Anyone who didn't read Amulet of Fire by Mr. Stone did not deserve to be eavesdropped on. I turned my head and listened to the people behind me. I was too curious for my own good. I felt like I could tell a lot from people's conversations. I would hear different conversations but the topics always seemed to be the same.

I got an orange juice and headed towards my shop. It didn't take me long to make my rounds. It was like a checklist in my head. Most of the items on my wanted list were still there. Some weren't and I'd either find them online or they'd be lost to the void forever.

The milk was easy to get. If I was doing my food shopping, I'd do it with headphones on. Shopping for food always overwhelmed me and there was just something vicious about the other shoppers in these stores. Their trolleys were their weapons and it would seem we were all fighting over the same foods even though there wasn't a shortage. With headphones on, I was at the whim of the song and someone could be blocking one side of the aisle while they were looking at products on the other half and I'd only want to sorta grab their trolley and just push it down the aisle and watch them chase it. Only sorta.

Although, the last time I was inside the shop with headphones on, I didn't hear the evacuation alarm and was escorted out after a tap on the shoulder. There might have been dancing involved. It had been a false alarm, but it was the kind of situation I could only shake my head in exasperation. Those sorts of things seemed to happen to me.

The bag was stretching at the weight of the milk. I mentally dared the bag to come apart and envisioned milk spreading across the walkway of the shop.

I saw an empty bench and quickly took a seat. Across from me was the electronics shop. I took the last remaining sips of my orange juice and watched a salesperson inside.

I couldn't read his nametag from the bench, but I was familiar enough with the store that most of the workers there said hello to me. Sometimes they'd tell me one of my tv shows had just come in with a new season. It was easy shopping at this store. The salesperson I was watching was named Greg. His charm was legendary, especially with me. His smile was usually met with getting what he wanted. He could rationalise choices and decisions. Customers would always ask for his advice on what they bought, what they had, what they wore, and who they dated. And I'm talking about myself here. Greg worked on me. I cared about what he thought. If he was displeased with someone I was wearing, I never wore it again. If I talked about a show I was getting into and he thought it was lame, that show was absolutely lame. I'd still watch it of course. He just never knew about it ever again. The best part about Greg was when he was extremely happy or excited about something that I was into. We'd talk for hours but in reality, it probably was only a few minutes, but I don't care. It was hours to me. I could listen to his smile all day.

He loved the attention. If he had become salesperson of the week again, I'd take a few of those made up hours of mine and stare at his picture. That charm though. I spent a lot of money because of him.

He looked out of the shop suddenly as if he knew I was thinking about him and winked. I blushed a crimson red and slowly stood up.

"Please don't make this awkward again," I muttered to myself and carried the bag of milk through the entrance towards Greg, who smiled and called out my name with the store's pleasant greeting attached to it.

As I grew closer and calling a greeting back out to him awkwardly, Greg eyed the display tables and cringed. He scratched the back of his neck. "What do you think? Too pretentious?"

"The greeting? No, you do it perfectly."

Greg laughed, "No, not me. The display."

Great, I thought to myself, I've made it awkward. "No, it looks fine."

"Are you still talking about me?" Greg grinned and I didn't have the money but I was prepared to buy whatever he had on that display.

Greg looked at the display for a bit longer and nodded, "I think you're right. It does look fine. How can I help you today?"

I blinked myself out of my stupor and stammered, "N-no. I'm just w-window shopping."

"My nan would always say that to me," Greg winked and I was ready to pull out my wallet and shove it into his hands and tell him to take me all.

"Good job, Greg," I said quietly and groaned. I might as well have said he was a good boy, scratched behind his ear and gave him a bone.

"Thanks. Been off my game today. Luckily I'm off now. Get to go watch Black Paper, finally. You seen it?"

I shook my head, "No, but I want to."

He wished me a good day and headed off deeper into the store. I quickly turned around and left. I passed the café and lingered at the cinema for a moment, staring at the poster for the movie before leaving the shopping centre.

I walked through the carpark and a voice called out to me. I looked around and saw Greg. He stood against his car. His keys were still in one hand. His other hand held my beating heart. His clean-shaven face held a dazzling smile. His eyes sparkled. His hair was perfect. His skin not too pale nor oddly tanned. His lips moved with his question but I didn't hear him.
"Sorry?" I said.

Greg chuckled, "I said, 'What about that movie? You want to go?'"

A Normal Day for
Benjamin Belmont Hastings

'It is an ordinary day like all the others.'

It's the same line I'd say to myself over and over again each and every morning.

It alleviated the stress.

I opened my eyes, slowly sat up and gazed up at the ceiling. 'It is an ordinary day like all the others.'

It's what I had to do. Already, I could feel my stomach tightening. I could feel my blood pressure rush through my body. Life was just so stressful, I thought. Getting out of bed alone was like jumping across a canyon. What if I stepped on the floor wrong? I began to picture things like twisting my ankle, chipping my teeth, cracking my nose and spreading blood everywhere, having to tear up the bedroom and replace everything, something going wrong with the repairs, a pipe busts loose and water goes everywhere...

'Stop it, Benjamin Belmont Hastings," I hissed and laid back down again, ensured the blankets were over me and started over.

I opened my eyes, sat up very slowly in bed so that I didn't hurt my back, gazed up at the ceiling to make sure that it was still there and whispered, 'It is an ordinary day like all the others.'

I took a few deep breaths. I didn't want to get dizzy. What if my blood rushed to my head and I fell over? What if I broke the lamp and caused an electrical fire? What if it spread throughout the house and I lost everything? What if I got trapped in my bedroom because as I rushed to the door I stepped on the floor wrong and a tiny muscle in my toe twinged and I lost a few seconds thinking about that instead of reaching the door and getting out alive?

I might have to call in sick.

I made the bed and choked on my words, "It is an ordin—"

I struggled to maintain breathing as I tried to control the cough. I decided I had said it enough today. I stood there like a soldier and inspected my bed thoroughly before turning ever so slowly and taking the exact number of steps I needed to reach the doorway. Anything more I might exert myself. Anything less I might strain myself.

As I started to walk out the door a thought danced in my mind until it became a dry itch.

What if there was still a crinkle on the bed?

I tried to ignore it. I knew it passed the inspection. I was so close to escaping my bedroom door. I only had 7 and a half steps before I could reach the bathroom.

'Benjamin Belmont Hastings, the bed is fine.'

I scrambled over to the bed and started over from scratch a few more times before the tears stopped and I was able to say, 'It's okay. It's perfect now.'

And it was. It was. It. Was. It was.

It's like the song says, 'don't let the sun catch you crying.'

I turned, humming the song loudly, took the steps I needed to reach my bedroom door without straining or exerting myself.

1. 2, 3 and 4. 5. 6. 7. A half. By the time I stepped through the bathroom door I was blaring the song out from between my lips.

The bathroom sparkled into my eyes and proved to me its worthiness of my entry. I was safe. I knocked on the door two times. You never know who could be inside. I entered and looked into the mirror and licked my thumbs and ran both across my eyebrows saying, "My, you're a handsome devil."

I kept saying it until I believed it or until the clock struck 7:20, whichever came first. If it was passed, 7:20, I called in sick.

Luckily for me, most days I made it and the clock always struck 7:20 first. I made a mental note to mention this at the counselling session next week.

I took off my clothes. I bent down to the bottom drawer and pulled out two rubber gloves. I placed them carefully on my hands, otherwise, I'd have to get another pair and that would be a waste.

I turned the shower on. The left nozzle went 360 degrees. The right nozzle went three quarters. The perfect temperature for a perfect shower. I undressed myself, changing my rubber gloves and stepped inside the shower and whistled, "Singing in the Rain' because one must always shower with a song.

I washed myself, making sure my eyebrows were shampooed thoroughly because I didn't want anything to fall from them into my eyeballs and scratch my cornea.

There's only so many times I can call in sick because I scratched my cornea.

After meticulously unwrapping my daily clothes out of the cling wrap, I dressed myself and headed to the kitchen where the coffee maker had already made my coffee. I opened up the blinds and realised my gloves were still on. I screamed as if I had seen a cockroach.

Perfect scream. Octave higher. Length adequate. A pinch of lemon juice after to heal the palate.

The juice would have to wait. I ripped off my gloves and had to go upstairs and dress all over again. When I came down, I cleaned the handle to the blinds. I looked at the time and shuddered in disgust.

I stood in my business suit and reached for my favourite mug. It was neatly placed next to the coffee spoon, which rested on a soft folded white napkin, that would soon be thrown away because I could only use napkins once, and if I were to have a second cup of coffee, I would have to get out a new one and neatly fold that one too and make sure it was at a parallel angle to the edge of the counter, which was neatly polished every night before I went to bed.

I took a breath. I had been holding it. For how long? What if I had suffocated? What if I died because I held my own breath? What if no one else had ever died like this before and so Benjamin Belmont Hastings became the first ever person to die because he forgot to breathe. I would spend my lunch break looking the statistics up.

I turned so that I was facing the blinds again. I made sure each foot was standing within its own tile. I sipped my coffee from the same spot. My feet were cemented in place. My mother had died years ago. It could have been from stepping on cracks. I would never know. I never got to ask and no one in my family would explain to me why people would say such things if stepping on a crack does not break anyone's back. They had no evidence that it didn't. And if this were true, why would anyone make cracks in the sidewalk anyway or allow to stay or create a tiled bathroom and then argue with someone for hours on end that carpet has no place in the kitchen. I know carpet has no place in the kitchen! Carpet has no place anywhere! They're just as bad as eyebrows! But no one can even suggest anything better than tiles because they all knew very well that wood panelled floors had even more cracks in them!

I felt myself unravelling again. I debated on whether or not I would have to call in sick but I still had time. I just had to reel myself in. I had to get back control. But how could I when things were rapidly falling apart around me?

Maybe I hadn't said it enough after all, 'It was an ordinary—'

The sound of someone screaming in absolute terror broke my concentration. I struggled to hold my mug. Wrong octave. Far too long and I would not share my lemon juice. I looked out the kitchen window and choked on my coffee as someone ran down the sidewalk. Their hands were covering their head as a flock of flamingos were chasing them.

They were screaming, 'I'm sorry! I'll never do it again!'

I blinked as the coffee dribbled out of my lips and back into my cup. I placed the coffee somewhere on the counter and took a blind step backwards. I probably killed a few mothers.

I reached for the phone and pressed speed dial, "I'm calling in sick. No, my corneas are fine. It was flamingos. Flamingos flew past my window."

The Princess of Delovia
Chapter Three
The Delegation

Casey pushed the door open to the Greetings Hall and took a deep breath before whispering, "Thank you, Your Majesty." He smoothed out his dress one last time and stepped through the main entrance.

He could have entered one of the many side entrances, but after leaving his bedroom, he knew he had to make an entrance. He snuck his way to the Alley, the large hallway that lead from the entrance to the castle straight through to the Greetings Hall, and slipped passed a few guards. Casey was able to use his hair to hide his face and he had never worn a princess' attire beyond the wing of the castle that his family slept in.

"They'll see," Casey whispered as he passed through the marble door frame and onto the landing that led to a set of stairs for anyone's grand entrance to see the Royal Family.

A servant approached. He was a tall man with a long snout that pointed more than it needed to up into the air, "Excuse me, Madame, but I must insist to know you so that I may announce you. Are you a part of the delegation?"

Casey used his fingers to delicately move his hair aside, "Yes, I'd like you to announce Princess Delovia."

The servant leaned over and his nose pointed directly at Casey, "Excuse me, Madame, but Delovia doesn't have a princess."

Casey took another deep breath. He just wanted to start walking down those stairs and greet the delegation.

The servant's eyes focused on Casey and the nose immediately pointed upwards, "Forgive me, young prince, I did not recognise you with your—I didn't know you would be—there's must be a mistake—this isn't a costumed ball, young prince—"

Casey nodded, "I am very much aware. Announce me as I have asked you to. Do not make me order it from you, please."

"Yes, young prince," the servant bowed and snapped his fingers to the other servants on either side of the door that were staring with large eyes and matching mouths. He hurried to the top of the stairs and called out, "I would like to announce the arrival of his young majesty Prince—I beg your pardon—I would like to announce the arrival of P-princess Delovia!"

Casey took one last deep breath as he descended the stairs and felt every eye of the room fall upon him. He felt the red velvet wrap around his skin and dance with his hips as he took each step. The blue satin sash swirled around him like the breeze fighting with the fallen leaves. He had held out a hand to be helped by the servant to walk down the stairs as Casey had seen other princesses do, but he found no hand to help him. He kept his back straight. His outright arm stayed there pretending to be holding onto a loyal servant. Casey kept his eyes forward, but they did not meet with others. Not yet. He wasn't ready to find eye contact. This entrance was about what they saw not the other way around.

The stairs seemed to clang like tiny bells as he took a step and for a moment Casey allowed his eyes to drop to his feet despite decorum. He grinned at the soft shoes that hugged his feet. They matched his dress and made him feel as if he were walking on air. That made the grace that came with the duty of a princess to come even more easily for him.

By the time he reached the bottom step, Casey knew it was time for his eyes to fall upon the others. Like blue crystal, his eyes sparkled across the room. He knew he had to great Queen Delovia first and when his eyes fell upon her Casey's grace almost faltered. His mother's face was twisted in both shock and repulsion. Casey nodded his head as he approached and forced his eyes to move away from his mother and to the group of men that stood in front of her. They were four of them. One of them was dressed in a complete set of shining armour. They stood silently behind a visor holding a staff with a flag on it. The other three were old. Most of them had strange moustaches. This must have been the delegation. The knight stood silently, the large visor facing Casey's way, holding a closed fisted gauntlet on one hip and clutching at the flagged staff with another. The three old men matched his mother's gaze. Lord Easton was behind them glaring at the other servants who were struggling not to laugh.

Casey opened his mouth and by clearing his throat three times, he was finally able to say the lines Lord Easton had forced him to remember, "Welcome to Delovia, Delegation of the King of Mandora. My father is most pleased that you have come to discuss the matters of our shared kingdoms. I will be

One of them stood in the middle at a monocle that had been frozen in front of one of his eyes for a moment before he allowed his to drop and raspy voice said, "Oh my."

The other two had long, bushy white eyebrows that furrowed together. They were almost identical except for the one with an extremely crooked nose, who turned to Casey's mother and hissed, "Are you trying to make a mockery of our visit?"

The other one growled, "His Majesty King Bartholin Rufus Mandora the Third will hear of this insolence!"
Before anyone else could speak to defend Casey, the castle shook with a tremendous roar. In the Greetings Hall it began to snow. Lord Easton ran towards the Queen crying out, "Your Majesty, with me! It's Bitemark!"

The ceiling of the Greetings Hall crumbled around them. Casey looked up but it was too late. A large blue claw swiped down from the newly made hole in the ceiling and swiped him up.

Casey screamed as the beating of Bitemark's wings deafened him. Wind whipped around Casey's body and tried to tear at his dress at the speed in which the fearsome dragon took towards the rising sun. The satin sash around his dress came loose and fluttered back down towards the castle.

The Knight in Shining Armour reached a gauntlet up and grabbed the blue sash that drifted from the hole in the ceiling and yelled, "We must rescue the princess!"

Charlie

The dark, crisp air touched their spine as they ran passed the old houses on Avenue Drive. Haunting pictures flashed before them. This street scared them. There was no avoiding the mystical road that reached their house. They lived down that dead-end dirt road five miles out of town. The council said it was supposed to be finished but things stopped even before they started.

Even after passing by the dying houses, they'd still have to shift through the forest, where a path of tire tracks led to their house. They hated those woods. The trees never let the sun shine through the cloudy green skies. Shadows lurked everywhere taking the shapes of everything that scared them. Why did the shadows hold so much power? They also hated their house. They lived above the church in a loft with their father.

The night owls asked them who appeared in the shadows. The birds asked them who they were, asked them who was behind them, asked them who they feared.

"I fear going home. I fear not being understood. I fear what my father would say. Would he talk to me as my pastor or as my dad? I also fear you," they whispered, heaving up their school bag against their shoulders.

They had to walk through the darkness that school caused.

School stole their daylight, so did the students.

"Charlie, Charlie, boy or girl," the students taunted them, "lumpy chest but has no breasts, is it a sock or is it a c—"

They pushed the voices out of their head and replaced it with equations. Maths always helped push away the cold.

They didn't drive yet. Their father said, "A walk through God's Country will do you some good, Charlie. Maybe even show you who you were born to be. None of this nonsense about not knowing what you are. I'll tell you what you are, Charlie, you are a child of God."

Their father brought darkness, too, which was ironic. They headed through the trees and could see the steeple first with its large cross starting to become hidden in the skies as the sun set.

For a moment, they stopped. The world seemed to be wiped clean of every living creature but them. They smiled. Alone on the earth. No one else judging. The only person right then and there was them and they accepted themself.

"I'm now the fearless one," they dared to say to the oncoming darkness surrounding them.

The wind scattered the leaves and startled them back into a quick pace towards their home.

The trees broke away and there the church stood in a clearing that had been created to pave way to God's Church. They had to destroy God's work in order to make it. The church seemed to thrive in the shadows as it sunk into its slumber. They listened to their breath echo throughout the trees. Their teeth chattered like falling rocks.

They tried to whistle a light tune, but their throat betrayed them.

The morning was much the same. The trees would hide away the sunrise. They'd smirk at the idea that the church started the day in darkness and ended in it, too. The words that fired out of the windows every Sunday made sure of it.

"Abhorrences!!" their father would scream out. They'd imagine the windows bursting outwards sometimes. "They cry out for equality! But the Lord made Adam first and then Eve! There is no in-between!"

The best part about the morning was that they were always walking away from the steeple and at one point was just walking through town. It was only when they'd turn away from the old homes, forgotten by the council as the town grew bigger and bigger, that they'd turn right towards the school and be walking towards darkness again.

"Good morning, Charlie!" a voice called out to them as they were just about to turn towards school.

They looked up and smiled, "Good morning, Mr. Dupoint. How are you?"

Mr. Dupoint scratched his bald head, "Just out collecting the paper but it doesn't seem to be here yet. You seen the Anderson kid?"

"No, Mr. Dupoint, I haven't!" they called out, "Sorry, I've got to get to school! Hope you get your paper!"

"Bye, Charlie!" the old man waved and they turned and headed for school.

The houses seemed to cringe with them. Groan at the idea that they were about to head to that school where they wouldn't even be able to get to the locker without someone chanting.

The smile they briefly had was gone, "I should have turned left."

Sam

The sun sent a warm feeling through my chest. It felt good to be able to sit outside without freezing. A cool air whipped around me occasionally like a small, playful child. My spine tightened as the breeze slipped down my back. The grass emitted a new aroma. The air had the right touches. It tickled me and my nose would sometimes feel funny.

Summer was coming. Summer would be when I'd be a bit freer. No more school. No more questions. No more shadows. No more being a grownup. I'd return to my summer job. I'd have freedom with my car. Not only would I get to deliver the papers in the morning but I'd get to drive away. I'd lie about my hours. Stay out longer than I needed to.

But this summer was going to be different. I was going to finally do it. Not like those other times in school during Maths Class or in the Cafeteria.

No, this time I was going to walk up and finally say, "Hi. I'm Sam."

I wanted Charlie. I wanted a summer full of Charlie. Just to be. To be free and myself and feel like a kid was supposed to feel. I wanted to go out during the day and play. I wanted to stay out late not afraid of the shadows around me because I wasn't alone. I wanted to be full of infinite energy again.

And I wanted to love. And be loved in return.

"Sam, get in here!" my mother's voice silenced the birds singing sweetly in the trees. She had that effect on people.

I itched my belly and looked down at it. It was all red and blotchy. I swore and grabbed my towel. I was trying to get a tan. It seemed like the more I tried to look good for Charlie the more I started to look bad. I needed to be my best version so Charlie had no reason to walk away from my, "Hi. I'm Sam."

I couldn't think of anything else to start off with no matter how hard I tried to be more eloquent.

"Sam!!" her voice made me cringe.

My mother said I was getting fat. I knew she was right. I knew she saw what I really looked like. I looked down at myself in disgust. My head was hurting. I gave a giant heave and fought against the sobs that wanted to come. I didn't want to go back into the house. I wanted to stay out and gaze over the old houses that surrounded me.

The birds in the trees gave short little tweets. They warned me about the shadows that loomed inside my house.

"I know. Believe me, I know, but what choice do I have?" I whispered back to them.

I stared at the glaring windows of my house. It hated me. I just wanted to stay out in the warmth. I wanted to explore the world around me and be a part of the leaves and grass. To be a part of Charlie.

Outside of my house, nothing ever judged me. Never abused me. During the summer, I got to take care of trees, the grass, the gardens and some animals. And in return, I felt like they took care of me. It's been happening that way all my life. But the shadows that lived inside my house didn't let me go.

I kicked the air. The wind picked up and loosened a few of the leaves from the trees. I'd need to water it. It had been so dry already. We needed a good rain storm.

I could hear the screams of my siblings. My mother's voice rang out again. Shrill now because I didn't answer her the first time and probably because I didn't answer the second time either. I held my breath. I took care of all five of them.

Charlie was an only child. That much I knew.

I opened my screen door and let it slam behind me. Soon ten hands were scratching at me. They pulled me deeper into the shadows. The glaring windows still watched me. They warned me not to leave like that again. The birds begged me to return to them.

Father's dark voice called from the depths of the living room, "Why didn't you answer your mother, Sam?"

The shadows from his doorway slipped across the frame as the hands dragged me further. Not even the shadows would take me in there. They led me to the kitchen, where a small window sat above the table where I had to put food. The shadows were hungry. They were always hungry.

The small window wanted me to leave. It showed me the birds dancing along the fence. The old houses waited for me to return so they could continue with their stories. I'd be late delivering the papers this morning and I only had myself to blame. I just wanted to enjoy the sunrise.

I gazed out the small window one last time as the sun disappeared and I watched Charlie rush passed my house. My heart leapt into my throat. If I hadn't have had to come inside, I might have had my chance.

"Hi, I'm Sam."

I watched out the window as Charlie stood at the intersection talking to someone before running off towards school. I wished they'd have turned left.

Black Paper

'That moment when everyone at school is suddenly talking about the best thing and you have no idea what they are on about. Fail. I get it when parents don't get things. Like, they're old and something about having kids just makes you lose contact with the cool things in life. My friends just look at me like I'm this virus now. My reputation is on the line here. What little reputation I have. Soon to be past tense. Come on, I need that book. I can't be the only Year 8 not to have read it. Help me, Bradley, you're my only hope,' Craig wrote quickly. His handwriting was awful and he was hoping it was still legible.

The book was supposed to be dark and mysterious. Urban legends were being created by this book. Apparently murders, suicides, and disappearances were linked to this foreboding piece of literature. He had to read it.

Here was the problem. Schools had banned this book from being stocked in their libraries. The public libraries refused to replace the books after so many thefts. It wasn't available online, and the bookstores weren't able to find a copy. It was as if it were out of print.

Craig would have preferred to have been teased about his sexuality, his eyebrows almost meeting, or the fact that he couldn't stop staring at Mrs. Miller. It was the ridiculous notion that not reading a book that would bring about the worst moments of his high school life. He even tried spreading rumours that he wet the bed, he picked his nose heaps, or worse, he couldn't fall asleep unless his mum tucked him in at night and sang him a lullaby. All those fake rumours somehow led back to the truth.

"Craig hasn't read the book," a girl in his class sneered.

"Do you even know what it's called?" an older boy he barely knew had asked.

"Yes," he blatantly lied, which had him chin deep in a toilet bowl. The truth was he had no idea what the book was called. The book was referenced, yes, but any mention of the title was changed. So much for Net Neutrality. The book was wiped off the face of the Internet. People claimed they knew the title but their posts soon disappeared. No one at school would tell him. It was just a big joke to them now. Craig started to wonder if most of them had even read the book themselves. His parents wanted nothing to do with it.

One day, however, Craig's life changed. It was a typical 'Let's Make Fun Of The Kid Who Hasn't Read The Book' day. He was at the end of a long line of ridicule, and when it finished, one of the boys stayed behind near the carpark where Craig waited to be picked up. Craig knew him well. It was Bradley Miller, son of Year 8's beloved English teacher, and he was holding on to a brown paper package.

"I got your note. You need to work on your handwriting," he said in his notorious deep voice.

Craig raised his eyebrow in response, "Yeah I know." He always found it hard to speak to Bradley.

"Like seriously it's really bad," he continued.

Craig sighed, "What do you want, Bradley?"

"To give you this of course," Bradley shoved the bag into Craig's arms, "It's a copy of the book. I stole it before my mum had the town burn it," his voice wavered a bit, and he wondered if he had heard Bradley's voice crack a little.

"B-burn it? She got the whole town? W-why?"

"You want it or not?" Bradley snapped and reached for the bag.

Craig pulled it out his reach, "Yes."

Bradley quickly walked away, "See ya, Craig."

He looked up to thank Bradley but he was already near the carpark and disappeared into the shadow of trees that bordered it, "Weird. Where is he going? He drives here."

The package seemed to burn in Craig's hands. He wanted so much to take it out and read it there, but he was afraid someone would take it or a teacher would destroy it. He decided it was safer to read it at home. He shoved the packaged book into his school bag, and waited for his parents to pick him up.

On the way home, he felt a strange warmth on his back. It was as if the book was truly burning, but Craig laughed at himself. He was just so eager to read the book.

It seemed to burn in his mind as he ate dinner, but once he found himself at the dinner table he found he didn't have much of an appetite.

"Are you sick? Do you have a test tomorrow?" his mum asked.

Craig made a face, "No and what?"

His mum raised her hands in defeat, "Nothing."

His dad added in between stuffing his face with food, "Looks like you and I will be having a night to ourselves."

He winked at her and Craig felt as if he had lost a second appetite.

He left the table, grabbed his bag, and dashed up the stairs.

Craig heard his mum say, "He took his school bag upstairs. I knew he was trying to get out of a test tomorrow."

His father replied, "Well he's going to cram, which means you and I have a date on the couch with our lips."

"Oh, you."

Craig shivered. The book could no way be darker and more mysterious than his parents.

He shut the door, almost slamming it, and put his school bag on his bed. He tore off his school uniform, dug into his bag for the brown packaging, and dived into the covers. His school bag bounced onto the floor with a thud.

He tore off the packaging and found a black book in his trembling hands. His eyes seemed to sink into the cover. It was that black. The title glowed in a brilliant white font.

Black Paper

He hugged it against his chest. Immature he knew but he felt as if he had been waiting all his life for this moment.

He slid deeper into the sheets, leaned over and pulled a flashlight out of his dresser drawer, and turned off the bedside lights. He swore he could still see the lettering of the title. His breath quickened as he pulled the sheets over him. He flicked the flashlight on and watched his belly heave in and out before he opened the book to the title page.

A letter dropped from the book onto Craig and he opened it up. It was written in panicky handwriting, "Craig, close the book and give it to your parents before it's too late."

Craig grunted. It must have been a warning from Bradley to scare him.

"Nice try, small fry," Craig mimicked something his PE teacher would say.

Craig flipped a few more pages with random warnings all written to him sliding out before he stopped at the page before the book began. He had to admit that his heart skipped a beat at the note taped on the page.

"I'm sorry. I always liked you. Goodbye."

Craig turned to the next page.

It was Chapter One. No subtitle, but it began on black paper with white font. The words glowed from the flashlight.

This book is written by itself. It holds no morals. It holds no purpose but to bring forth your fears. I must warn you to beware. This book holds the darkest of evils. Most likely, you won't finish reading this chapter, and by then, it'd be too late.

Craig raised his eyebrow. Was this it? It was written like a poem. Center of the page and the font seemed more written than typed. Craig raised an eyebrow. Though he wasn't scared yet, his curiosity had his legs continuously move and his eyes were eager to read more. He couldn't stop smiling. He was still thrilled, and couldn't wait to boast about it at school. He continued.

It begins, lifeless and without form, a mere shadow in the back of the mind, twisting around the brain's curvatures, as if they were the roots of the gnarled tree out front. The tree is alluring; its branches reaching to the stars begging for mercy.

With each unspoken word, the shadow rises against the breeze, once peaceful now shivering, and steals it for the shadow's breath.

It always begins this way, never outside but from within.

And from this shadowy idea a creature emerges forth. The dirt of the earth spoils and all life from within wilts. It is but a glimpse of a peripheral eye against the wall.

It is normal to fear it, child.

After taking its first breath from the breeze, it takes its first step: an important one. It gathers its strength from that step, like a turn of a page.

Craig turned the page.

After that step, the creature glides across the ground like your eyes reading this page. It is drawn to the warmth in which its power derives from. It hates the warmth. It would be siphoned.

The front door lingers nearby it. The frame frosts over and cracks. It is a touch of death, which forms its heart. Like your mouth, child, the door opens in anticipation. The creature's heartbeat your own. You know what's coming. You were warned.

Within. The creature is within, as two warmths share a moment together. Their lips are dark and mysterious to the creature. It is blinded by it, and it is enraged. As its touch nears, the warmths attempt to move closer. This is when it strikes. It tears them apart. The woman first. The man second. Their flesh becoming its flesh, gnawing, scraping, all with silent screams.

But it is not finished. There is still a warmth. It lingers beyond its reach for now. The creature lets out a loud rasp. It bathes in the scent of their cold lifelessness before rising up the stairs. The creature is covered in the parents; their weight causes each step to scream the screams the parents were not allowed to share. It nears the last warmth it needs to destroy.

Craig lifted his head up and held his breath. His hands rested on either side of the book. He thought he had heard the creak of the stairs outside his room. He sat there and listened but heard nothing. He let out his breath quickly and returned to the book.

The hallway is hollow. Its claws stretch out to either side as it fills the space the pictures tremble. The walls whine. The handle to your door rattles.

Craig froze. His eyes stared down at the words but they dared not read them. One hand now clutched the flashlight. The other had his heart. He could hear the actual sounds the book was describing. He heard his door open. It was his parents. It had to be. The book couldn't be describing him. His eyes scanned the page further.

It arrives.

The creature's shadow looms above your sheet, child. You do not realise that it is your parents upon it; their blood a pool in your living room. It finally releases the shivering breeze into your room; its claws descend towards the outline of your head beneath the sheets. I warned you, Craig.

Craig closed his eyes. Doubt stopped his scream just as fear had stopped him from reading further. As he opened his eyes, he allowed them to travel upwards. His body shivered from fear and from a cold draft that seeped into his sheet. He wanted to scream so badly.

A shadow loomed over him. His eyes snapped involuntarily shut, and he whimpered, "I don't want to read this book anymore."

The sheet was torn off him and fluttered in the breeze like black paper.

The Princess of Delovia

Chapter Four

Bitemark's Tower

The Knight in Shining Armour stood there and watched the others deliberate and fawn over the Queen of Delovia. Stewart, the ambassador of Mandora, was whispering quietly to his counterpart, Fineas, who was cleaning Stewart's monocle. Lester, one of the sages of Mandora was busy ensuring the Queen was safe.

The ride on horseback to Delovia was tedious for the Knight. Stewart had debated all the way to the kingdom on whether the King of Delovia was fit to lead. Fineas had of course agreed with the eldest of the trio. He always agreed with Stewart. It was Lester who the Knight respected the most.

Lester snapped the reins lightly until his horse caught up with the lead, "Stewart, we mustn't be too hasty. I shall request to attend to King Delovia myself. Surely, I am equipped with the necessary condiments for what ails him. We are stronger united. Not apart."

Stewart sniffed, "I've heard that there's more than just a cough that ails this royal family, Lester. Not even the strongest sage can cure the young prince for what plagues him."

The Knight's gauntlets tightened on the reins and pulled

back slightly until the horse slowed. The only think the Knight could hear now was the raspy chortle of Fineas.

As the Knight listened to the gripes of Stewart and Fineas about how the attack of Bitemark was a sign that this trip was indeed foreboding of their alliance's future, the Knight's gauntlets imagined tightening around reins once again and moving away from the ambassador and his eager butt-kisser and moved closer to the sage.

Lester held the hands of Queen Delovia, "There appears to be no scratches or marks. Though you seem out of breath. I might suggest you retreat to your quarters and allow yourself some time to breathe. Deep breaths I tell you. Five in a row. Through the nose and out the mouth."

"Thank you, Master Sage," Queen Delovia struggled to say between trying to catch her breath. "Lord Easton, see to the servants. Get our guests some refreshments. We will reconvene. In a more suitable room. Might I suggest. The High Council's room? They were going to meet. With us shortly after. The greetings anyway."

A man, the Knight assumed was Lord Easton, bowed, "As you wish, Queen Delovia."

Lester held the arm of Queen Delovia, "I really must insist you rest for a moment."

The Queen nodded and began to move away from them. Two servants rushed up to her and replaced Lester at her arms. "Thank you, Master Sage."

"Please, Your Majesty," the elder sage bowed his head, "Call me Lester. I am only here to serve." He grabbed something out of one of his pouches and put it into the hands of one of the servants attending to the Queen. "Make a tea from this. Wait for it to brew for a few moments. Then she must drink it. All of it. The cup must be clean afterwards. See to it."

The servant nodded and was just about to exit out of a side door when the Knight called out, "Excuse me if I'm speaking out of line, but what of the Princess?"

The Master Sage turned to the Knight and rushed back over, placing a wrinkled hand on the chest plate.

The Queen paused for a moment before leaving the Greetings Hall without another word.

Lester cleared his throat, "Nevermind that. Bitemark would have torn him asunder by now. Though chivalrous. Misplaced."

"So, no one is to do anything?"

"These matters are complicated."

The Knight's visor clanked as the helmet shook back and forth, "No. Something must be done."

Lester watched as the Knight in Shining Armour turned abruptly and stomped out of the Greetings Hall. The staff with the Mandora flag on it was snatched up into a gauntlet. The end that held the flag was snapped off and Stewart or Fineas could say anything, the Knight in Shining Armour was gone.

A crowd had started to gather outside of the castle as the Knight weaved through the questions and the gawking. The stables were not far from the entrance and upon approach a stable boy had seen the Knight coming and had begun to prepare a horse.

The Knight ruffled the boy's hair, "Thank you. Tell me where I'll find the blacksmith."

After the stable boy gave the Knight directions, it wasn't longer after that the horse was dodging pedestrians as the Knight's heels dug into its side. The horse snorted its lack of appreciation but did what was asked.

The blacksmith was at his anvil arguing with his daughter when a horse suddenly galloped up to the workshop and the Knight in Shining Armour slid off and started marching towards them.

"I want to learn our trade, father!" the daughter demanded.

The blacksmith gaped at the Knight approaching behind her.

"Are you listening to me? I want to be a blacksmith! You know I'd be better than you!" his daughter shouted until she fell into a whisper as the Knight swiftly walked passed them to a rack and pulled off a sword.

"I shall be needing this. Please seek out the Master Mage in the castle to retrieve your compensation." The Knight swung the sword a couple of times on either side of their armour before hitching the horse and pulling back up onto the saddle. The Knight called back out to the blacksmith, "This sword is fine craftsmanship. Did you make this?"

The blacksmith, stunned into silence, shook his head and pointed to his daughter.

The Knight nodded, "You are correct. You will make a fine blacksmith," and the horse rode off as quickly as it had approached.

The blacksmith's daughter slapped her father's arm, "I told you," and in a mocking tone of her father said, "But no, girls can't be blacksmith."

The blacksmith nodded again and pointed to the anvil, "Let's begin then…"

The Knight's horse galloped fiercely through the rest of Delovia, only stopping once so that the Knight could grab a bag of rations.

"I am riding a couple of days to the Frosted Mountains. I need enough rations to get me there and enough rations to get two people back."

The woman stood there wrapped in a shawl staring at the tall, Knight in Shining Armour. "That will be 12 coin, but are you sure you want to go there? Bitemark is said to live there. None return!"

The Knight climbed back up onto the horse and called down to her, "Seek out the Master Sage in the castle. He will compensate you for your generosity. I must go and save your princess!"

The woman's mouth dropped open and she cried, "But we don't have a princess!"

The Knight in Shining Armour road for days. During the night, when the Knight fell asleep on the saddle, the horse would take these moments to stray just off the path to eat, find water and sleep standing up. By morning, the Knight would awaken to the gallops of the horse as they both grew closer and closer to the foot of Frosted Mountains.

A single farm lay just off the road leading up into the

frozen mountains. The Knight slowed the horse down to a stop and slid off. The Frosted Mountains were glazed in snow. The peaks were hidden somewhere above the thick whiteness.

"Good day to you!" a voice called out and the Knight in Shining Armour led the horse to the farmer and made an agreement that the horse would stay there until the Knight's return.

As the night came and the temperatures dropped, the Knight in Shining Armour grew fearful not of the freezing temperatures but for the Princess and whether Bitemark had already devoured the poor damsel in distress.

By the sun's rising and the temperature, the Knight in Shining Armour followed the treacherous trail all the way to the peak of the mountain. Two caves opened up like hungry mouths. One at the end of the trail. The other closer to the actual peak where the Princess stood at its cliff edge.

"Knight in Shining Armour?" the Princess called down.

"Don't worry, Princess of Delovia, I'm here to rescue you!"

And with that a mighty roar came out of the mouth of the cave and the Knight in Shining Armour drew out the blacksmith's daughter's blade and shouted, "Prepare to die, Bitemark!"

Geneva and the Other Daughters

Once there was a man with seven daughters. He would say he loved each one equally and his daughters believed him, but his wife, Alma, knew the truth. There was one daughter the man loved more, above all the others. In fact, her sisters loved her the most as well.

Her name was Geneva.
She was not beautiful by any means, nor strong in stature. In fact, Geneva was quite weak and would be prone to illness. Alma would find herself taking care of Geneva most days and grew to resent her. The other daughters would coddle her. The husband would work harder to pay for the salves from the local witch.

After many years, Alma grew tired. She lost all reasoning as to why she took care of beloved, Geneva. All she could think about was the years she had given of herself and lost. Soon her love was replaced with bitterness and blame. She began to believe that Geneva had stolen her life away from her.

Soon, Alma started to question her husband's love for Geneva and devotion. Wasn't it her that took care of her husband's every need? Was it not her who took care of all seven daughters, but most of all, was it not her that took care of Geneva? Where was her praise and gratitude?

When would she get all the recognition?

One day, a gnarled woman appeared at the family's well in front of their house and spoke of a rare gem that could not be found anywhere in all the land. This gem was so sought after and coveted that even the witch desired it so much so that she vowed to do anything to get her hands on it.

Geneva and the other daughters listened to the story of the rare gem, but it was Alma who quickly started to scheme. She wrote a letter to her parents, who were merchants and did trades from across the seas. She waited months before she got a reply parcel and in it was the rare gem. She was disappointed for it was as plain as Geneva. Just a gray stone with no shine. She snuck out one evening with the gem in her cloak's inside pocket and delivered it to the witch.

"I am most pleased, Alma," the old witch exclaimed at the sight of the stone, "How did you get your wicked fingers upon this delight?"

Alma grinned at the witch, "It does not matter. I have it and now you do. I was told by a gnarled woman at my well that you would do anything to get this gem. Is this true?"

The witch bowed her head, "Unfortunately, this tale is twisted. I will admit that I have longed for this stone. It was a cure for a disease I have been fighting against for years."

Alma waved her hand at the witch, "I do not need your reasons. I just need your word. Will you do whatever I want for this stone?"

The witch smirked, her eyes twinkled, "I believe I will, Alma. Just for you."

Alma laughed for the first time in years, "Then I ask you be rid of my daughter, Geneva, so that I shall be the most beloved woman in my household once again."

The witch paused for a moment, thinking on this request. Her eyebrows arched until suddenly she snapped her fingers and nodded, "Now give me the stone, and your request will be completed."

Alma dropped the stone in the witch's gnarled hands. The witch laughed and quickly ran over to her cauldron and dropped the gem inside. Her words rose up and echoed throughout the hut:

"Daughters love all that their mothers say,
and if they don't their hearts turn away,
mothers be proud that you each share a bone,
or one day soon you'll be the only woman standing alone."

The witch turned to Alma and without looking dipped a red ladle into the boiling mess and sealed it inside a vial. She scampered up to Alma with frightening speed and with a twinkle in her eyes again, said, "One sip is all it will take, Alma, and the daughter you see before your eyes will vanish."

"One sip? And Geneva is gone?"

The witch smirked, "Then all will fall at your feet the love in which you deserve."

The mother raced home quickly and found her family getting ready for bed. They were each giving a kiss to Geneva's forehead. Alma slipped into the kitchen, her lips held fast to her secret and made a pot of tea. As she listened to the spoon clink against the teapot as she stirred,

Alma stared at the vial in her other hand. She wondered where Geneva would disappear, too. What would happen after? Alma would of course fall into despair. Her husband would do all that he could to support her. The other daughters would faun over their mother. Alma would act so grief stricken that soon the attention would be back on her. They'd applaud her for her efforts in trying to take care of Geneva. Alma grinned.

Alma tapped the spoon on the lip of the teapot before opening the top of the vial and adding just one drop into the tea.

"Alma?" her husband called from the doorway and so startled was she, the vial dropped into the tea. "What was that?"

She put her hand to her heart and stared down at the tea before putting the lid onto the pot, "I went to the witch. It is a tea for Geneva."

Her husband suddenly looked hopeful and nodded head, "Here, let me help you, my darling."

Alma blushed at the sentiment and put the teapot on the tray with a cup and saucer and handed it over to him. He disappeared out the kitchen while she tidied up. She took a deep breath and pretended to be full of sorrow when he'd come running back and say Geneva was gone.

There was a shatter of porcelain against the floor and Alma dropped the towel she was using to clean the kitchen and rushed to her daughters' rooms.

The tray was still clattering against the floor and tea and porcelain was everywhere. She looked around the room.

At first, she thought it was empty but from behind the other side of the bed a gander and seven geese waddled out to her.

Alma took a step back. The gander walked around the geese, six were white, and one was gray.

The witch's words echoed in the room:

"Daughters love all that their mothers say,
and if they don't their hearts turn away,
mothers be proud that you each share a bone,
or one day soon you'll be the only woman standing alone."

For a moment, remorse almost broke through her bitterness until her eyes fell solely on the grey goose, "Even cursed, simple Geneva, you stand out amongst beauty."

Geneva waddled up to Alma and began to cough until at Alma's feet clattered one dull grey stone.

Milk With Your Coffee

I sat down at a table people seemed to avoid, but I didn't care. I needed to sit down. It was empty and it was clean and after the mess of a day I was having I needed as much cleanliness in my life.

I sipped my Frappuccino, grateful that my credit card still worked. As long as I got a job soon, I'd be okay. Life was just full of setbacks and getting fired from my last job was still a bit of a shock.

A few people looked my way for a brief moment before averting their eyes and walking away. I tried to hide behind my large drink. I began to wonder if my zipper was down, but why would they be looking under the table. I mean, sure, maybe that's what people do often and I just didn't realise it. I quickly checked my zipper. It was fine. I wondered if I had chocolate chip between my teeth. I ran my tongue along my teeth. Something was upsetting people because the more he looked around the more they gave these looks.

After a few awkward seat adjustments, I realised it was directly at my table they were looking at but somewhere behind me. I turned and looked and my eyebrows arched up as high as a barista does when you explain your butt isn't padded.

A woman was sitting there with a towel draped over her shoulder, covering a little infant suckling at her breast. I smiled fondly and turned back around. If that was what people were freaking out about then they needed to get over themselves. It was a sweet moment between a mother and her child.

I sipped at my drink and let myself relax into the chair until I heard a voice behind me complain, "Must you do that here? It's disgusting! I'm trying to eat!"

I quickly turned around and watched an elderly woman call out across the café to the mother and her child. My eyebrows scrunched together.

"Excuse me?!" the elderly woman called out again and the mother looked around and realised it was her the woman was talking to, "Must you do that?"

The mother's face grew read and she adjusted the towel more than she really needed to. I grew angry for her but the mother snapped, "My child needs to eat, too."

I nodded my head at her and looked to the elderly woman. I had to say something. This mother needed support. I mustered up some strength and called out, "Yeah, she's doing nothing wrong! Leave her be!"

The mother looked at me and smiled. I sat up a bit higher in my seat and turned back around. I did a good thing. Perhaps my day wasn't lost after all."

"Oh really, this is unacceptable," I heard the elderly woman snap, "Where's the manager?"

I whipped back around. The mother just rolled her eyes and adjusted herself once again. She didn't look like she was going to say anything and no one else came to her aid. The elderly woman was getting up and seemingly heading to the mother's table. I had to intervene.

"Lady," I called out, "Just mind your own business. You're eating. The child is eating. We all are having a nice beverage. It's a beautiful moment."

The elderly woman got to the table of the mother and I stood up, "She's doing nothing wrong. If anything, you disturbing the rest of us. If she wants to pull out her boobs and feed her child that's her right. There's nothing wrong with her boobs. It's beautiful."

The elderly woman froze and the mother looked up at me, "Excuse me?"

I smiled at the mother, "No seriously, you keep ignoring her. She's the one with a problem. I quite enjoyed turning around and seeing you breastfeed."

The mother quickly adjusted herself to where she could begin to button herself up.

"Are you a pervert?!" the elderly woman suddenly snapped at me.

"Who me? No! Just because I support a woman breastfeeding her child? There's nothing wrong with it. Just a child enjoying a nip at her nipple."

"You're disgusting," the elderly woman snapped.

The mother looked at me, "Sir, you need to sit down. My breasts are not for you to voyeur."
Suddenly, I grew very confused, "I was just sticking up for—"

"No," the elderly woman snapped, raising a hand up to me to get me to stop, "You need to leave." The woman looked down at the mother, "Are you okay? Is he making you uncomfortable?"

I took a step back. What was happening? What did I say? I looked between the two and looked around the café. The barista threw down her towel and started making her way from behind the counter.

I repeated everything that I said through my head, "No, you don't understand. I said the moment was beautiful. Not your breasts. Not that your breasts aren't beautiful. They probably are. I'm just saying that the moment between you and your child was beautiful. I was supporting you!"

The barista approached me, "Sir, you need to leave."

The elderly woman sat down next the mother and ogled the child, "I'm so sorry little one. This man is disgusting. Don't you worry. We'll take care of you."

The mother snapped at me, "Just leave."

She had buttoned herself up and put the towel away. The elderly woman had the child in her arms now cooing a finger against its cheek. I stood there dumbfounded before the barista stood between me and them.

I walked away and sipped on my Frappuccino but it gurgled. I looked down into the cup and saw that only the cream was left. I dropped my drink into the bin on my way out.

The Author of 'The Amulet of Fire'

He stared at the aisle in absolute terror. He'd already popped one Valium. He was tempted to take another. Flight 452 had given him a window seat. He had requested an aisle seat. He had made it perfectly clear that he was claustrophobic. He needed room to move. He needed the option to get up and roam if he needed to roam. Instead, he'd have to crawl over other passengers. He scanned the rest of the plane. It was crammed. His brow broke into a sweat and he chewed on one of his fingernails. He closed his eyes.

He stood at the edge of Paradise and gawked at the view. The expanse of the sky above was like a great swirling ocean of soft clouds. The Valley of the Zabobo Trees, purple leaved trees native to Paradise, spread across the land like soft pillows. He clutched at the amulet in his left hand and raised it above his head. This was it. This is what he had been waiting for…

"Sir?" a voice broke through his thoughts. "Sir? If you could please take your seat, sir. Mr. Stone?"

He slid into his seat without another word. He hated confrontation as much as he hated closed spaces. He slid open the window cover and closed his eyes. He needed to travel back. He needed to be somewhere else besides crammed next to the wall of the plane. He needed to return to Paradise.

This is what he had been waiting for. A chance to redeem himself. This simple action would change everything. All he had to do was throw the amulet into the Valley of the Zabobo Trees and…

"Excuse me?" a voice tore through his refuge. "Excuse me? Did I hear the stewardess correctly? Are you Mr. Stone? Mr. Stone the author?"

He took a deep breath and a switch in his brain went off. He opened his eyes and put on a bright smile before reaching out his hand and nodding. The young man shook his hand eagerly and continued to ramble on about how much he was a big fan. He heard it all before in the most inconvenient places.

One conversation took place over a partition of a cubicle. It was as if his fans seemed to forget social etiquette and boundaries. He never complained, but he did refuse to shake the hand with the gentleman in the cubicle. Besides, didn't he want this fame all his life.

"Thank you so much," he smiled again, shaking the young man's hand far longer than he needed to before he returned to his seat. He just needed a moment. One moment to collect his thoughts without having to take a Valium. But, it didn't look like he was going to be able to. He slipped a hand into his jacket pocket.

"Wait!" a voice cried out to him as he was about to toss the amulet over the edge. "Don't do it!"

He turned and found himself facing Prince Adol, the future king of Paradise. He had hoped he would have thrown the amulet over into the valley before the prince had caught up with him. He had underestimated him once again.

"You don't know what you are doing, do you?" Prince Adol pleaded, "Once that amulet falls into that valley, everything changes."

"It's the price for freedom," he said strongly.

"Is being ruled by my family so terrible? We've enslaved no one. We have not taken freewill away. You throw that amulet into that valley and the borders of Paradise will dissolve. What could possibly be out there worth that?"

"Mr. Stone?" the young man had returned, this time with a paper and pen.

Mr. Stone blinked a few times and the sweat formed on his brow again. He took a deep breath, muttering to himself, "I just needed a moment..."

He stopped himself and eyed the young man, "I'm sorry. You just wanted a signature?"

Something faded in the young man's eyes. Mr. Stone sighed. He had let another fan down.

"Sorry," he stumbled again, "flying makes me nervous."

"Oh, yeah, me, too," the light returned into his fan's eyes. Mr. Stone quickly signed the paper before the young man was rushed to his seat by the stewardess.
Mr. Stone was about to close his eyes again when his chair jolted a bit and a little boy was pushed from the aisle into the seat next to Mr. Stone. The mother nodded at her small son as she put her carry-on into the upper compartment and sat down in the aisle seat.

Mr. Stone looked at her longingly, wishing he was sitting in that seat instead. She said something to a man across the aisle and kissed him on the cheek. The man winked over at the little boy. He then eyed Mr. Stone suspiciously before recognition struck him across the face. He hurriedly whispered something to his wife, who turned around in obvious shock.

Mr. Stone turned away embarrassed, but the fasten seatbelt sign distracted everyone. The plane was due to depart.

He rushed away from the prince and leaped into the wide-open expanse above the valley.

The prince screamed out in horror from the cliff, but it was too late. The prince watched as his last hope free-fell into the purple sea of leaves. The amulet was still clutched in the hero's hand, even as the branches began to beat at his body and break him...

The explosion shook the whole plane and Mr. Stone woke. His hands quickly tugged at the seatbelt before they planted themselves on the armrests. Screams erupted louder than the actual explosion. Voices over the intercom failed to calm everyone. The world around him began to slow; however, the plane plummeted towards the ocean. He felt each jolt as if they were branches from a tree slamming into him. The screams tore through him. He couldn't think. He couldn't stop the world around him.

The plane jerked again as it tried to blast its way through the water. The water was stronger. The air spun around him. His heart pounded in his ears. He could no longer hear the screams. Panic was taking over. He tried to cry out, but his mouth refused to stop grinding.

One last jolt sent the seats slamming into each other. Another eruption of screams roared like a raging storm as the chairs pinned the passengers to their seats. The spinning stopped and the sinking began. Madness set in. People began to claw at their legs, at their seats, at each other.

Mr. Stone looked out his window. The ocean was coming fast. He could see it. He could feel it around the plane. He could hear it call to him. It didn't take him long to see it engulf the people several aisles away. People were desperately trying to swim towards an exit before they vanished into the mouth of the sea. It was hungry.

He felt a cold hand grip his. He turned and blinked away the panic.

The little boy's eyes looked up at him as he said, "I'm scared."

Mr. Stone nodded and looked into the boy's eyes. He could see hope dying.

"I'm scared," the boy repeated, his lip trembling. His eyes filling with tears. Hope was drowning, just like they soon would be.

Mr. Stone looked over to the boy's parents. They were clawing at each other trying to pull each other out of the clamped chairs. The mother randomly would try and tug the boy out before turning back to the husband begging for help.

Chaos was in control.

Mr. Stone shook his head and leaned over as best he could to the boy, "No. You shouldn't be. You never should be scared. You know why?"

The boy's tears began to flow down his face. A soft moan was beginning to creep out of the boy's mouth.

Mr. Stone shook his head sternly, "No. You know why? Do you?"

"No," the boy squeaked.

"Because you are the bravest…"

…Knight of Zabobo. The most frightening thing in all of Paradise could not scare the young Knight. He lived in the deepest part of the Valley of the Zabobo Trees and watch over all of Paradise from there. Legend has it that the knight could sense when terror struck across the land, and he would only then leave his home to face the terror and destroy it.

The screams slowly faded away as the ocean took them. Hopeless silence began to seep through the trapped prisoners of Flight 452 as the gurgle of the ocean seemed to laugh at them. The more the ocean took, the more the others in the cabin could hear Mr. Stone.

"What did the knight do?" the boy begged.

"Well on this particular day…"

The Knight of Zabobo had seen a man leap off of the highest cliff of Paradise and tumble down right into his backyard. Normally, any small boy would be scared to see this terrible tragedy…

"But not this boy," the little boy added.

"No, certainly not this boy…"

The water grew closer.

The Knight was not afraid of death. Paradise didn't believe in it. None of the people had to face it, unless the borders of Paradise were to fall, but that would never happen. Only the Amulet of Fire had the power to destroy the borders, but the amulet didn't exist anymore. So, the knight thought, until the body fell onto the ground and the amulet rolled over to him.

Mr. Stone could see the young man straining to look back at the author as he told his tale loudly. The mother leaned against her son quietly sobbing. Mr. Stone winced for a moment as the pain from the chairs pinning him shot up his body.

"Go on!" the young man called back to him.

Mr. Stone looked around. All eyes were pinned on him. They avoided the terror of the hungry waters. Some had their eyes closed, but begged for Mr. Stone to keep talking.

"Do not be afraid because the man who fell did not die…"

The boy knight was very wise for his age. He knew that if the amulet were to break within the borders of Paradise all of the people would lose hope and happiness. They would have to face sickness and death once again, and he knew what he had to do. He scooped up the amulet and vanished.

"Where did he go?" the boy asked.

"No one knew," Mr. Stone shrugged, pointing to the boy's arm, "until today."

The little boy gasped, "Me?"

Mr. Stone nodded, "Yes. You. You are the Knight of Zabobo, who protected the Amulet of Fire until he one day returned with his new army."

Tears formed in the boy's eyes, "But I don't have it. I lost it."

Mr. Stone shook his head. The ocean was beginning to swallow the young man.

Mr. Stone leaned over to the boy, "but, Sir Knight," he urged, "don't you feel it? It's in here." Mr. Stone pointed to the boy's heart.

The little boy closed his eyes and nodded.

"Knight of Zabobo," Mr. Stone asked, "should we be scared?"

"Save us!" someone else sobbed.

"I don't want to die!"

"This can't be happening!"

"God, HELP US!"

The little boy opened his eyes and looked up at Mr. Stone before turning to his mother, "Do not be afraid for I'm the bravest boy in the whole world."

"GOD!" voices began to rise up in panic once again.

"I'm the Knight of Zabobo!" the boy cried out, "Do not be afraid for I am with you!"

The young man vanished quickly and Mr. Stone felt the sting of death seep into his shoes. He looked at the wall that rushed towards him. Panic rose into his throat as a whimper squeezed out of his teeth.

A small touch soothed him. He turned his head to find the little boy looking over at him.

"Is Paradise as beautiful as I've dreamed?" Mr. Stone asked the Knight of Zabobo before following him into his world.

The Knight of Zabobo opened the gate to Paradise and smiled, "I think so."

Behind the Hedge

She smiled. Her headphones plugged into her ears, which vibrated with music. One thing was for sure. It certainly inspired her to dance. Her cheeks burnt slightly. It wasn't like she was somewhere private or in the anonymity of a club. She was sitting in solitude, certainly, but only by a hedge. Anyone could walk around it and besides, she knew her playlist. If the right song popped up, she would most certainly stand up and use the surrounding patch of grass as her dance floor.

She didn't mean to always exclude herself from society. Headphones. A corner in a library. The trees outside of town. A hedge. But the whole point of putting on the headphones and drown herself in the illusion of surrounding silence was to find inspiration. It guided her decisions. It tapped into her creativity and allowed her to be as if no one else was looking.

She kept her eyes closed. It allowed herself to see the music. She let her head nod slightly. Her imagined her heart beating along with the music and every now and then she'd thrust her chest out slightly. Her toes tapped against the soft grass. Her shoulders swayed. She needed this. She needed this moment. This space in between life where she could just drift between life's sounds.

She stood in the illusion of her solitude and danced.

She chewed at her bottom lip. She could feel the smile spread across her face as a part of her lifted into the air and spun slowly around in the moment. She could feel each note. The tone. The change in beat. When it flattened. When it sharpened. She felt it all vibe through her ears, resonate in her head and spread through her body as if it were sheet music.

The song ended but with a push of a button it fell back into repeat. Her whole body was on repeat. Repetitious motion. She wasn't ready to return from this escape. In this moment, between this song, she was alive and it was all the reason she needed.

She could see herself as if she were above, dancing among the clouds that leapt through the blue sky. Music, she could repeat. It wasn't as fleeting as a perfect moment in time. A dinner. A passing stranger with a great smile. Helping a friend. Each of those moments were unique. A different time and a different day. But this song, despite the fact the sun and the clouds kept on moving and tilting and wilting away, she was listening to the same song with the same lyrics within the same music and it brought the same feelings. Music was her déjà vu.

The song still on repeat. She felt as if she were the instrument. She was the one that that danced on the wall. She forgot about the hedge and the solitude her closed eyes gave.

A tap on the shoulder brought her spiralling down from the clouds and slamming back into the reality of the soft grass, the tall hedge and the sun that now danced overhead.

She shrugged her headphones off and put a hand over her eyes, "Oh, hi, Charlie. Sorry, was just listening to some music. Glad you could make it. Ready to get this assignment done?"

Charlie chewed on a nail, "Sorry about disturbing you."

She avoided eye contact and waved the comment off, "Don't worry about it. I told you to meet me here. We're just waiting on—"

Footsteps through the grass stopped her and she turned around to see a hand reach out to Charlie, "Hi. I'm Sam."

The Princess of Delovia
Chapter Five
The Prince Isn't Getting a Ball

Casey watched in silence as the cold wind blue at the red dress with the blue, satin ash and Bitemark battled for its life against the brave Knight in Shining Armour. Within moments the skilled hero vanquished the dragon and scaled the cave's treacherous climb until Casey was found up in the nesting ground of what belonged to the frosty dragon.

Casey leapt into the Knight's arms and kissed the cold visor, "My hero!"

The Knight let gravity pull her out of the freezing gauntlets and back onto the ground, "Oh, well, of course, Princess Delovia, it was an honour."

Casey blushed, "You may call me, Casey. After all, you did save my life."

The Knight lifted up the steaming visor and Casey's hand and kissed it quickly before the visor slid back down with a clank, "You honour me more, Casey."

The Knight in Shining Armour wrapped Casey up in a warm shawl that had been stuffed in a sack that hung off the Knight's shoulder.

"I believe this belongs to you," The Knight said, holding out Casey's blue satin sash. Casey smiled and wrapped it around the red dress. It matched the shawl.

Inside the bag there was also food and drink that made Casey feel warm all the way back down the mountain where a farmer waited with the Knight's horse.

They road back in silence as Casey held tightly to the back of the Knight, both of them grateful to have escaped the cold of the mountains. By the time they returned to the Kingdom Of Delovia word head spread of the Knight's brave deeds. The delegation awaited their arrival where Casey was surprised to see King Delovia himself sitting back upon his throne. The moment that Bitemark had been defeated the curse had been lifted.

The Knight in Shining Armour was hailed a hero. Casey watched as the royal family crowded him with the delegation standing nearby with stilted pride.

"That's fine," Casey muttered, "I'm okay. Thanks for asking. I'm fine really but thanks for worrying, mother, father…oh, by the way, father, it's good to see you alive. Oh, yes I'm glad to be alive, too."

King Delovia, thankful that his cough was now gone, loudly proclaimed, "It is with deepest pride that I announced tonight we will celebrate the Knight's return and the defeat of Bitemark with a ball!"

Everyone in the Greetings Hall cheered, everyone but Casey. He found himself under the nose of Lord Easton sneering down at him, "Come, my Prince, we must find you suitable attire. It's time we rid this Kingdom of all curses."

Casey followed, giving one last look to the Knight in Shining Armour.

Read the Books

I had time to spare before work. I liked being early rather than being late. I'd slip into the library. It still had dim light. His boss hadn't turned all the lights on yet. She would be in the back typing on her typewriter. He could already hear the dings. Her computer was in the corner collecting dust. There was another one in the middle office where I could catalogue all the incoming books. I was pretty sure I was the only one using it.

I also liked to come in early so that I could read through some of the newer books. I'd read the backs of them. I'd also thumb through the magazines. Sometimes I'd do it as I was cataloguing them and waiting for their stickers to print out or while I was putting the security tape on the back page.

I liked to read things because, well first, I liked to read, but also because I liked to help. People would come in looking for a particular book or ask suggestions for a new read and I was able to help them. It made me sound like I knew what I was talking about even if I hadn't had the chance to read a great book. Okay, I'll be honest. I also liked the idea of reading a new book and if it was really good, knowing that I was the first to read it.

I'd boast about it sometimes, "Yeah, I read that one already.

It was a great read."

No one seemed to have a problem with me reading except for Rosie, my boss. I had been only working there a few days and I was used to her clearing her throat and asking, "What do you think you're doing?"

I looked over at the printer. It still wasn't done printing so there wasn't much I could do but wait, besides, the library wasn't open to the public yet.

"I'm reading this article," I said, "Did you know that belly buttons grow special hairs to grow lint? Like, is this a new evolution? Mutated hairs because humans created lint. Like what about the Neanderthals who didn't have polyester cotton ironed shirts like ours?"

Rosie pushed her lips together. I only had been working there a few days and I already knew that I had to close that magazine fast and pay attention. She had things to say.

"You are here to catalogue the books. To print out the barcodes for the books. To stick the barcodes in the books. To mark the books with the security stickers and to place the books out on the floor where they are supposed to go."

I nodded, "I know."

"You are not here to read the books," she'd snap and return to her back office where I'd hear her madly typing a way followed by some pretty angry dings.

I started to listen out for her keyboard. As soon as those dings would stop, I'd close the books or magazines and stare intently at the printer. She'd slowly walk out of her office and eye me. She'd almost circle around me before slowly nodding and returning to her office.

The problem was when I was scheduled to be at the front counter. It wasn't a hard job and I was pretty good at it. I'd wait for the public to come. I'd serve the public. I'd walk around the library if there were people cruising the shelves and offer my assistance and if there was a cart full of books, I'd return the books back to where they belonged.

I also read them.

Sometimes someone would return a book and I'd ask them about it. Especially if it looked interesting. Then they'd leave and if it really peaked my interest, I'd give it a bit of a read before I checked it back in or even better, as I checked it in.

But Rosie seemed to have this seventh sense about her. She'd know when I was at the counter reading and like an old lady ninja she'd sneak up behind me and clear her throat. The hairs on the back of my neck would rise and I'd slam the book shut and turn around.

"You are here to catalogue the books. To print out the barcodes for the books. To stick the barcodes in the books. To mark the books with the security stickers and to place the books out on the floor where they are supposed to go."

"Yep," I needed my head, "I know."

"You are not here to read the books," Rosie snapped, "How many times must I tell you this?

I think I am the first person in history to secretly try to get away with reading a book in a library.

I devised a plan. As I was pushing the cart through the library and disappeared between the shelves to return the books, I'd sneak a read through the magazines. I felt like I was doing something entirely devious.

"Oh, I'm so naughty," I whispered, "I'm reading a book in a library."

This guy grunted and left the aisle we were sharing.

Sometimes when someone was returning a book and boasting about how good it was, I'd casually look around after they left and call out, "Oh look, there's no one else here I might as well return this book now."

I'd sneak away and pretend that I wasn't sure where it went and start to read it quickly.

For a few days, I got away with it, it seemed. But then Rosie started to appear at the end of the aisles. She'd catch me reading a book and I'd blush and put the book away or scramble away and return it to where I actually knew it belonged.

"You are here to catalogue the books. To print out the barcodes for the books. To stick the barcodes in the books. To mark the books with the security stickers and to place the books out on the floor where they are supposed to go. You are not here to read the books."

"I'm just trying to do research to what the public like," I tried to argue, "You know, customer service."

"Do your job," she hissed and stormed off.

The thing is I was doing my job and I was doing it well. Too well in fact because it got to the point where I'd have free time and the books would just call to me. Begging me to read them. To touch their pages once again. My mouth watered at the thought of books that's how hungry I was starting to get.

"Just let me read the book!" I suddenly snapped and the person at the counter gasped.

"I'm sorry is that book reserved?"

"Oh no. No no. I'm just not allowed to read."

"But you work in a library."

"Try telling that to the librarian," I muttered and checked their book out for them.

I had been working at the library for two weeks. People were starting to remember my name. We'd talk about certain books. Some of the moms would gossip with me about the magazines. Some of the dads would, too. And even though I wasn't into many things they weren't into, I enjoyed hearing them enjoy it.

Rosie didn't seem to enjoy it. In fact, it became quite clear that Rosie didn't enjoy me. At all.

I finished off the last of the barcodes for the magazines when I read aloud one of the headings of the magazines. It shocked me, "Tragic end to The Amulet of Fire."

I heard a throat clear itself from behind me and I spun around, "Did you read this?"

"No, but apparently you did," Rosie snapped. "You know. I've been good to you. Your job was simple. You catalogue the books. Print out the barcodes—"

"Oh, I wasn't reading, Rosie, I just read the heading," I began to explain.

Rosie spoke louder, "—on the books! Then, all you had to do was stick the barcodes—"

"I know but if you'd let me…"

Rosie's volume increased, "In the books! Mark the books with the security stickers and place the books—"

"Yes, but," I stammered, "I was just shocked to read…"

Rosie yelled, "Out on the floor!! It is so SIMPLE!"

"I know and I am…"

"And all I ask," Rosie suddenly went calm and my whole body shivered, "is that you don't read—"

"…the books," I added in defeat.

"You're fired."

"What?" I gasped, "I work in a library and I'm getting fired for reading?!"

"Goodbye."

Chad's Assignment

"Whacha writing?" Chad hissed as he plopped himself backwards into the chair in front of her and snatched the notebook out of her hand.

"Chad, give it back," she sighed, resting her chin on her hand. She refused to play his little game and try to reach for it. He'd just pull it out arm reach and find pleasure in her insistence.

"Gonna read it in front of the class again? I'm sure Mrs. Miller would love it."

A couple of other boys sat on either side of Chad. Their faces already held looks of amusement. She rolled her eyes and didn't hide it.

"What was it you wrote last week? The Princess of Droolicious?"

"Delovia," she snapped, "It's not that hard to remember."

"Right, right," Chad nodded, pretending to be interested as he twirled the notebook upside down, "So what's this one? I can't read it."

The other guys laughed. She just stared ahead to the front

of the class just waiting for Mrs. Miller to come in and start the class. Chad would change his tune. He acted tough but he was terrified of their English teacher. He certainly wasn't her favourite.

"Aye, Chad, you got it upside down," one of his goons laughed, pointing out the joke she should have.

Chad looked over at her and flashed his pearly whites, "Oh yeah. Silly me. Guess I was distracted by your beauty, Sal."

"Oh, gawd," she groaned and rolled her eyes again. Mrs. Miller stepped into the room for a moment before pausing and turning around to talk to someone. Probably her son.

"The Trail of Smoke?" Chad read aloud and that's when she quickly reached a hand out to it. Chad pulled it out of reach and laughed, "I see a trail of smoke coming from you every day, Sal, cuz you're so hot."

Sal gritted her teeth together, "Give it here, Chad."

Mrs. Miller called out as she walked across the front of the room to her desk calling out, "Alright, where did we leave off? And Chad, that better be your assignment because I'm not in the mood to deal with your procrastination today. And sit in that seat properly before I make you sit on the floor."

Chad stood up, "Yeah, Mrs. Miller. I have my assignment right here," and winked back behind him and whispered, "Thanks, Sal."

She hissed, "Chad, don't you dare," before sinking lower into her chair.

"It's called," Chad said in an exaggerated foreboding tone,

"The Trail of Smoke."

His goons all in a deep voice went, "Ooooh."

Mrs. Miller sighed and sat down at her desk, "Alright, Chad. Let's hear it, but if it's another one of your speeches as to why marijuana should be allowed at school, forget it."

Chad scrambled to the front of the room and jumped in place. He grinned, "Oh no, this is going to be good. I dedicate this one to Sal. Hey, babe."

She glared back at Chad and muttered, "Why are guys like this allowed to exist?"

Chad flashed his pearly whites again, "They stood at the edge of the forest…"

134

The Trail of Smoke

They stood at the edge of the forest and gazed over at the trail of smoke that plundered somewhere beyond the field that lay before them. The clear, blue sky has become a gray expanse. The three friends took another step out of the trees together. Two of them held each other closely while they watched the smoke pillage the sky. The other one glanced a few times before turning his sights back to his hands.

"What do you think it is?" Joseph asked, as he held his girlfriend in his arms. He kissed her forehead before unwrapping his arms around her and taking another step into the field. He noticed his clothes were covered in a thick layer of dirt. He patted his shoulders but it didn't seem to do anything. He looked over at his friend and grunted, "Ty, quit playing with that thing and take a look at this."

Tyrone pushed the power button on his mobile a few more times. It hadn't been working since they stepped out of the forest. "Yeah, I saw. Not sure, but the reception sucks out here. It can't be my battery. I had it plugged in the USB port in the car."

Alicia wrapped her arms around her the moment Joseph stepped away. She noticed a few leaves were entwined throughout her hair and began to comb her fingers through. No matter how many times she brushed it, more leaves seemed to be there. She sighed, "How we get way out here? Where's the car?"

Both boys shrugged.

"We pulled over so I could pee," Joseph confirmed, "right?"

Alicia began to frantically pull at the leaves from her hair, "It's not going to rain is it? I didn't bring an umbrella."

Joseph took a deep breath and gazed up at the grayness. It hurt his eyes. He coughed a bit before saying, "Maybe. Hey, you smell that? I think I can smell the smoke from here."

Alicia and Joseph stared at the trail of smoke across the field. She wrapped her arms around herself tighter, quietly wishing Joseph hadn't let go.

Joseph coughed, "I can taste dirt."

Tyrone didn't even look up from his phone as he continued to play with the buttons, "Smoke doesn't taste like dirt. Wait, can it? Soon as my phone is working I'll look it up."

Alicia shivered as a slow wind howled through the trees behind her. She whispered, "I'm so cold," hoping Joseph's arms would return around her.

"Where there is smoke there is fire," Joseph suggested, "how about we check it out while we search for where we pulled over?"

"I don't even remember getting out of the car. But I did. And we were walking through that forest," Alicia rubbed her arms and frowned, "Where did we even stop?"

Tyrone waved his hand in a random direction, "I dunno. Somewhere over there."

Joseph rolled his eyes and began to walk across the field. He patted at his clothes again to get rid of the dirt. It was beginning to bother him that it wouldn't go away. Alicia followed, rubbing at her neck and shivering. Tyrone blindly followed as he continued to fiddle with his phone.

"Joey," Alicia whimpered, "when we get back to the car can you give me a neck massage? I think I slept on it wrong."

"Yeah, sure," Tyrone joked, "When you 'fell asleep' in his lap. We know what you were really doing."

Alicia grumbled, "Don't be gross, Tyrone."

Joseph fought back a small cough, "Ignore him, babe, boys are gross. I'll look at your neck when we get back."

As they crossed the field, the sky dulled even more. The plume of smoke thickened and they noticed fire flickering in the horizon.

"See," Joseph wheezed, "fire. Man, a lot of fire."

"Isn't that the road?" Alicia pointed to the edge of the field, "Wait…"

"Holy shit, Tyrone, is that your car?"

Alicia shivered, "Oh my God, it is, Ty. Look!"

Tyrone looked up from his phone and swore. He shoved it into his pocket and rushed forward. Raging words blasted out of his mouth. His car was lodged into a thick tree. "What the hell, man?" Tyrone screamed, "Who did this?"

He patted his gray jumper pocket and stomped his foot, "Oh my God, I'm so stupid. I left the keys in the ignition. What the hell, man?"

"Dude, your cars burning. Your keys won't help," Joseph called out at Tyrone ran towards it.

Alicia rushed after Tyrone, who was already as close as he dared to his car. The blaze was still roaring. Alicia followed the flames of the fire up the tree as it licked through the branches.

Tyrone, "My dad is going to kill me. How could I be so stupid? Joseph, why the hell couldn't you have waited to pee when we got home? Oh, man, you just wanted alone time with Alicia. What the hell, man?"

Tyrone ran his hand through his hair, "Who would do this?"

Alicia stood just beyond the fire, rubbing at her neck and shivering, "I want to go home."

A wrenching cough came from the side of the road where the smoke played with the loose gravel and dirt. Joseph's voice rose from within the mixed clouds.

Alicia called out, "Joseph, don't get too close? What are you doing?"

"We did this," a voice called out from the trail of smoke.

Tyrone swore, "What you on about, bro? No way are we completely responsible!"

Tyrone circled the car until he reached the driver's side. He could hear Alicia calling to both of them to come back away from the car. He could hear Joseph coughing up a storm from the other side. His eyes widened as he saw a body hanging out from the window of the driver's side.

"Oh, man, who is that?" Tyrone choked, "Hey, buddy, you do this to my car?!"

"Ty," Joseph gagged.

Alicia screamed, "I want to go home!"

Tyrone backed away, "Oh I think this poor bastard is dead!"

A head hung loosely out the window with an arm outstretched clutching a phone.

"Poor bastard probably was trying to call for help," Tyrone called out to the other two. He took a few steps sideways to get a better look at the face., Eyes stared back at him but they could no longer could see. Tyrone ran his hands against the side of his face and up through his hair. Same colour. Same pierced left eyebrow. A half-burnt jumper matched the gray of the sky.

Tyrone stumbled backwards until he fell over something. Dust swarmed around him and he found Joseph coughing uncontrollably nearby. His eyes staring in fear at the body Tyrone had tripped over. Tyrone's mouth dropped open and he scrambled away, "Holy shit!"

A body lay half buried in the dirt. A trail of glass led back to the car.

Tyrone screamed a screamed that match Alicia's. He jerked

his head over towards her. She stood near the tree gazing up at a body hanging by their own hair from the branches. Their neck twisted like the gnarled bark of the tree.

A truck swerved off the road suddenly. Its tires spinning to a stop in the dirt. A man and his wife jumped out of the vehicle quickly.

"Honey, call the police!" the man ordered.

She was already on the phone but scrambled to the half-buried body of a young boy in the dirt. She pushed away the dirt from the face and gasped in horror before she looked up at her husband and shook her head.

He scrambled to the car just as flames burst through the driver's window and engulfed the young man holding onto a phone.

He looked over at the tree and tried to warn his wife not to look, but her scream hinted that it was too late. They both scrambled back to their truck and held each other tight as she gave instructions to the emergency operator.

"I love you," they both whispered to each other as they watched the trail of smoke disappear into the blue sky.

Talent

"…watched the trail of smoke disappear into the blue sky," Chad finished, licking his dry lips and clearing his throat. He slowly lowered the notebook and looked up at her. "That was brilliant, Sal."

Mrs. Miller slowly stood from her desk and reached for the notebook, "As I suspected, Chad, you didn't do your assignment. Again."

Chad allowed Mrs. Miller to slide the notebook from his hand as he made his way back to his seat in silence.

"Salwa," Mrs. Miller walked up to her and held out the notebook, "I believe it's you we need to thank for that gripping story."

A few of the students giggled at the mention of her name and Chad slammed his hand on the table, "Shut up, okay! She's talented. Salwa is talented."

Salwa squirmed in her seat but took the notebook quickly as Mrs. Miller winked at her and whispered, "I told you you needed to share your stories more. Don't let them silence you."

Mrs. Miller returned to her desk and spoke loudly, "Alright, who's next with their own assignment? Don't make me go down the list!"

One of Chad's goons sneered back at her, "Beautiful story, Sal, you the girl in the tree?"

Chad slammed the back of his hand into the goon's chest, "Shut it, stupid. It was good. Leave her alone. Unless you got a better story."

The goon rubbed his chest and faced forward as Salwa bowed her head and flipped through her notebook to a blank page. She hadn't wanted it read. It would only point out how different she really was to the rest of the class.

A tattered green notebook slide across her blank page and she looked up to see Chad quickly turn back around.

A torn page marked where she opened it, the ripped message said, "It's only fair…"

And Salwa read the page. Tears began to form in her eyes. She panicked as a few escaped and landed on his page, but she could see the tear stains already there. Her breath caught in her throat as she nearly finished and as the last line sunk in to her heart like a dagger, she quickly flipped the torn page over to its blank side, stuck it into the notebook and tapped it on Chad's back.

He turned around, a worried look on his face as he took it back and she heard him open the notebook. His hand suddenly shot up into the air, "Mrs. Miller, can I be excused?"

Mrs. Miller waved her hand at him as she encouraged the student in the front to continue and Chad took that as a yes as he quickly crossed the room, slipped out the door and leaned against the hallway's tiled wall. He opened his hand where he had crinkled the note and read it again.

"For someone who is talented, too, you waste it all by being a jerk."

Chad hung his head in shame, "I know."

144

The Princess of Delovia
Chapter Six
And They Lived...

Casey entered the side entrance of the Greetings Hall scratching at his neck. The collar of the terribly stiff, gray suit felt like sandpaper. He still had refused the tie much to Lord Easton's protest, that was until Lord Easton returned with King Delovia's insistence.

Casey felt his throat tightened with each gulp of air. He felt exposed even though the suit covered him completely. As he snuck through the guests of the ball, they greeted him as was due but he still heard the whispers. After all, this was the Prince who wanted to be a Princess. The shame of Delovia. One who is so late to the ball that the Queen herself refused to have him announced.

Lord Easton had sneered as he tightened the noose-like tie around the Prince's neck, "You must understand, my Prince, the servants just don't know what to call you anymore. Now that your father is back in his throne, you must return to his regime. Under his thumb and his guidance, you will be the prince you are meant to be. Enough of this nonsense. You were merely grieving over the loss of your father. The Knight in Shining Armour saved this kingdom from two curses."

Casey had pulled away from Lord Easton and had stared coldly into the mirror at the imposter that reflected back at him until he had freed himself from his own gaze and had looked up over at Lord Easton, "Let it be known, Lord Easton, that I absolutely loathe you."

Now, Casey found himself avoiding finding his place up near the thrones. If they weren't going to announce him, surely Casey would get away with admiring all the beautiful gowns and gorging himself with food and drink.

Casey stood at the end of a banquet table closer to the entrance when he found the crowd starting to part. Casey took a deep breath and rolled his eyes. His mother must have spotted him, which meant they would insist he take his place front and centre for everyone to see that they indeed had a normal prince who would one day take over Delovia.

Casey turned away from the crowd and stuffed his mouth with a cinnamon roll. He refused to go elegantly.

"I've been looking for you all night," a voice cut through the music.

Whispers spread throughout the crowd and the music suddenly faded. Casey could hear his father on the throne asking what was going on and Lord Easton vowing to find out. Casey also heard his heartbeat in his throat and a suddenly ringing in his ears. He knew that voice.

Casey turned around and with a mouth full of a cinnamon roll tried to say, "My Knight," but it came out with a splatter of half-chewed roll and sounding more like, "Muh Nigh."

Casey's face turned beat read but a laugh echoed the Greetings Hall, "May I have this dance, Your Highness?"

Casey struggled to swallowing, giving the crowd enough

time to spread their whispers as the Knight held out a gloved hand and Casey took it. Once the cinnamon roll was gone, Casey replied, "I thought I told you to call me Casey."

The Knight laughed again and Casey found his heart bouncing between his chest and his throat with each laugh. "May I have this dance…Casey?"

Casey felt himself being pulled out into the middle of the floor which became empty instantly as everyone made room for the pair.

"What are we all waiting for?" Casey heard his father snapped, "Start up the music!"

The Knight pulled Casey closer and they both glided across the floor for a few moments before Casey felt the warm breath of the knight against his ear and the hint of lips, "You look good in that gray suit."

They spun around a bit more and Casey tried to pull away. He didn't want to be dancing with the Knight like this. It wasn't what he was picturing the moment they stepped out onto the dance floor. This is not how he pictured himself falling in love.

The Knight pulled Casey a bit closer, not letting him escape, "But, Casey…"

Casey attempted to pull away one last time until the Knight practically kissed his ear and whispered, "I prefer the red dress with the blue satin sash."

148

Just Be

"I can help, mommy," Billy had said, as his mother struggled to carry the laundry basket to the door. His father, in his stained wife beater and oiled jeans pulled at his ear until Bobby had returned to the living room. "No son of mine will be acting like a woman!"

Billy stood on the hill of his family home. The trees that seemed to never age waved at him in the distance as the sun rose above the horizon. Two poles stood on either side of him a few arms lengths away. A weathered clothesline draped between the two. His father had only replaced it once. Billy would soon have to replace it again. He stared at the clothes as the wind helped dry them. His long hair blew in the wind. He grabbed at the hem of his dress so that it didn't fly over his head. The neighbours didn't need to see his underwear.

He laughed at the irony of that thought as he looked over the clothes once more and then at the trees and the sun over on the other side of the hill. He thought of his mother fondly. The laundry baskets and the cooking. The cleaning and the crocheting. The movies that made them cry. The men they found beautiful. And the men that they did not…

He thought of the day his father died when Billy's mother

came up to him after the funeral. She sat next to him on the very couch he had grown up to hear how men should be. She reached out and touched his hand. Caressed his cheek and said, "Now you can be the man you are meant to be."

Billy stared at the pair of red shorts that hung on the line. A voice called out to him and he turned around to see his husband wave at the backdoor. A little boy stood next to him hugging his father's leg in a blue shirt and undies. He was waiting for his shorts to dry. He would wear nothing else. Billy grinned and let his hem go as the wind took this opportunity. His dress fluttered upwards a moment and they all shared a laugh.

"I am strong. I am independent. I am nurturing and kind. I am free," Billy whispered, as he returned to his family, "I am woman."

Beneath the Shorts

"Go put on your shorts." Mrs. Miller, Lakewood High School, 1995.

Not only was I starting high school for the first time, I was also returning to school after being forced to finish a majority of Eighth Grade at home. This was enforced because the Middle School couldn't cope (didn't want to deal) with the extreme bullying that was happening to me. So, the adults in my life decided it was best for me to finish my schooling at home. They'd send school work home with my brother.

I returned to the same problems in a different school. After all, the bullies got to finish their school and I didn't. I was put in classes that were for lower graded students. My grades from Eighth Grade were low and incomplete. I came from a low economic home. Mrs. Miller was my English teacher and within weeks, she realised that I was ahead of the students, despite having almost a half a year away from education.

Mrs. Miller tried to help with the bullying. Her classroom became a quick refuge and her excitement with my writing inspired me to write more and more. I'd finish many of my assignments quickly. The problem with her classroom is that it only had four walls and her power did not expand to the hallways. I'd walk into her classroom with a distressed look on her face.

One day she walked up to my desk where I was quietly crying and rubbing my chest where I had just been punched. She tapped it and whispered, "Go put your shorts on."

I immediately laughed and asked her what in the world she was talking about and she kneeled down next to me and explained that she'd set a timer and I had to write her a short story from start to finish before the timer was up. At first, I didn't succeed in her challenge but soon I'd rush to her class not only to avoid the horrors that waited for me in the hallways, but because I wanted to finish her challenge. She wouldn't say it every time I had her class, but mostly, she'd say it when I finished my work early and satisfactory.

I didn't know what to do with my collection of short stories. Some of them I'd get to read out to the class. Other times I'd just keep them for myself or give them to Mrs. Miller as a gift. Mrs. Miller always challenged me and pushed me to try new things. In school competitions. Newspaper competitions. I never won the in-school competitions. The awards went to the popular kids. I never really got to enter the newspaper ones because there usually was a fee involved. But I dreamed of putting together all my short stories and selling them to help my family. Maybe I'd stop my dad from being angry all the time. Maybe my mom would be safe. Maybe I'd be safe to walk down a hallway. I would call the collection: Shorts. I thought it was funny and clever.

There are two stories included in this anthology. Both of them were written in Mrs. Miller's class while a kitchen timer ticked away and no one in the class knew it was entirely for me.

Go put your shorts on.

When I Had One Job

This story is absolutely true. I call these moments "Mike VS. The World" where I get so caught up in doing and saying the right thing that I get myself into a bit of a mess. I get so scared of offending people or what they think of me that I pre-emptively try to fix a situation that just didn't need to be fixed. Just off of High Street in Penrith, Sydney, I was trying to find a job while I was going to university to finish off my teaching degree. Though the job agency no longer exists there, every time I pass by the building I remember the door and the sign attached to it. I see the window I leaned on to try to catch my breath only to realise I'm pushing my butt up against the glass for all inside to see. I was mortified.

I know why I get myself into these situations but I just don't know how. What triggers me to suddenly be afraid about what the other person is thinking? There are quite a number of stories in this book that are derived from my Mike VS. The World moments. Perhaps you already have ones in mind that could possibly be true.

When I Met Montley and Mr. Benedict

I had a neighbour. I'd pass by his house on my walks with a smile because I knew what I'd see. I'd see him and his wife tending to their garden. They had a row of roses she'd be pruning. He'd have his wheelbarrow handy and his trowel would be digging on either side of the bushes. They were always extending that line of flowers. I'd wave. They'd wave. Sometimes she'd call out to me and tell me to wait up a moment as she snipped a rose off and brought it to me.

"For that special someone," she'd say with a wink and we'd ask each other how things were. I'd get updated on the neighbourhood whether I liked it or not.

I once said to her, "I don't have anyone special at the moment."

She just laughed that comment off and said, "But you're special. Always saying hello and chatting up the little old ladies."

Then one day, she was no longer out there. Neither was he. We all knew why. We all mourned together in the neighbourhood. She was something special and I had wished I could wave hello to her just one more time. I'd deliver a rose to her and say, "For that special someone."

Her special someone stayed in the house. I'd see the blinds part sometimes when I walked. I'd wave and the blinds would close quickly. I knew he needed time to mourn. We all did. But days of mourning turned to weeks turned to months turned to years and I learnt that mourning someone wasn't as easy as getting over it.

Sometimes we never do.

I watched as the roses faded away from neglect. I heard that some people from the neighbourhood had tried to help but he insisted they be left alone. I wished I could click my fingers and have his love come back. Grow in full bloom.

But like most things in life, I had no control over his hurt. He lived in that house, behind those blinds, for as long as I lived there. I probably triggered him but I couldn't help it. I did it more for me anyway, let's be honest. I bought a rose. I left it on his doorstep with a card that simply said, "For someone special." And then I moved away.

Later, I'd create Montley as a homage to both of them. Mixed into one. But also added the element of what someone might go through when they live behind a blind. Perhaps he still talked to her.

I know I did every time I walked past.

When I Wrote Hidden Hills

Originally this story was just the poem. I wrote this poem as I finished my degree in Primary Education when I should have been paying attention in my Introductory to English lecture. I always imagined my grandmother as Milly. Like most of my writing I didn't know what to do with it and besides, I felt like it needed more. So, I tucked it away into the pile of poems, short stories and starts of novels that I still have to this day.

Almost a decade later I came across the poem again. It was like visiting with an old friend. I remembered the class in which I wrote it. They were explaining adverbs. Ms. Faggan. She was a firecracker and I loved every snap and crackle she brought into my life. I needed an elective and hers was the only one available. She wondered why I didn't take the advanced courses and I had said they weren't available.

"You're definitely a writer," she'd wink at me and slap my ass. She was a short little thing and always said she couldn't reach my hand so my ass was closest. We got each other's sense of humour and so I didn't mind my ass getting slapped by her. No jokes, a few of the students thought we had a thing going on.

I asked her why she knew I was definitely a writer and her reply, "Because you have trouble with time management. Apply for courses early, you dumbshit."

She was pretty amazing.

As soon as I found that poem and returned from memory lane, I knew exactly what to do with Milly Cloud. It was a perfect bedtime story and I was working closely with a friend of mine. She was a painter and sometimes if we were online at the same time, I'd catch her putting her son to bed. It was a cute dynamic watching the little firecracker avoiding bed and giving me perfect inspiration to give Hidden Hills that little extra that it always needed.

When The Rock Met The Roll

This was another little tale I had put together in Ms. Faggan's class and why it's put in a similar format. A tale within a tale but this time I included the character Montley, as well as putting a few more secrets in that would link to other stories included in this anthology. "Montley" and I would always bump into each other at the library. I was there to borrow the next book in the series of Hardy Boys, The Baby-Sitter's Club and Nancy Drew. They were there to either read to the kids for fun or she'd be borrowing another romance novel she thought I never noticed in her hands.

This story in particular was when Ms. Faggan caught me writing in her class instead of paying attention. She had asked a question and I had missed it. No one in class could answer it so she turned to me. I didn't hear the question and so didn't come up with the answer. First few times I actually made her frown until she talked to me after class and asked me what I was doing. I showed her the tale.

"I hate it," she snapped and threw it back at me.

I'll admit I was cut pretty deep. She must have seen it on my face because she continued quite quickly, "The roll is a little shit. Like I get it. She doesn't want to be eaten. You know what, I don't want to get old. But here we are."

I grinned.

"And the poor rock. The poor wind. Here they made a perfectly good deal and got what they wanted out of life. But that damn compassion gets in the way. I say let the roll get all gross. At least she would have lived!"

"Like you accepting you're getting old?"

"Listen you little smart ass, this isn't about me. And I'm not turning hard and gross and I smell like petunias."

There were a few more expletives in what she had said but that was Ms. Faggan. She told me that I could continue to write in her class as long as I let her read them afterwards. It became another English class I found refuge in.

"Mike, we're talking adjectives today and since you're one big one yourself, I expect a story by the end of this hour that will knock my pink socks off or you're failing my class."

But, with more expletives.

When I Was Creamed

Sadly, but for your amusement, this story is partially true. Another Mike VS. The World. Except the truth is I was with colleagues of mine. It was a Friday afternoon and I was invited out for a coffee. I was so excited about my life at that point. Hyperactive in that my teaching career was blooming and I wasn't going to be going home alone on a Friday night wondering why no one loved me. I'm babbling with the other teachers. I'm making them laugh. I got paid. Bills were all caught up and I was getting out of debt. Plus, we were being served by a barista that already knew my name. Knew what I liked. Made her laugh as well. It was a perfect moment.

Until things unravelled quickly when the barista asked, "And do you want cream with that?"

And I blurted out loudly, "Yeah, baby, just cream us all!"

Too loudly. Like, the café seemed to go silent because I was that loud. The barista snorted as she tried to stifle her laughter and I went into panic mode and tried to explain to the whole room that I didn't mean sperm.

Needless to say, a few of the staff dragged me to a nearby table and told me to shut up.

When I Rode A Spy Train

Here it is. The first. This story is the godfather of everything you hold in your hands. Your eyes have read an anthology of stories because of the paranoid thoughts of a train farer. Besides minor edits and a bit of updated language and sentence structure, you are reading the story I wrote in Mrs. Miller's class back in high school. The timer was going and all I had in my head was the sound of a train as it sped down the tracks. I wrote in a frenzy and that frenzy turned into the character's paranoia as he started to spiral out of control from the anxiety that kept building.

When I read Spy Train, I don't see the story but I see myself sitting at the desk in my own frenzy. I'm writing it quickly. His madness my own as we reach the inevitable conclusion of the timer dinging and I'm throwing my pencil down and grinning.

Mrs. Miller told me in the next class that her and her family had all been laughing at my story.

"You read my story aloud to your family?" I suddenly felt extremely nervous.

"Only the good ones," Mrs. Miller winked, "And so that's pretty much all of them."

I started thinking about the train, how it stops at different stations and that's when I started forming my idea for a collection of short stories that would be like train stops to different parts of the same line. Mrs. Miller and I worked on getting it together and preparing it for submission. But sadly, the real world got in our way. The bullying was increasing. I wasn't getting the same opportunities as others were in school. I kept getting in-school suspensions because of fights or arguments. And by fights, I mean, the students were hitting me. Sometimes I defended but that was rare. And by arguments, yes, I'll admit to those. I'd argue with teachers, especially when they sided with the bully.

I'm happy that I get to do another thing for the younger version of myself. A gift to me. Here's this idea you had, young Michael, that you never got to complete because life wasn't fair. But it was all meant to be because, let's face it, some of those stories you selected to put into your collection, just weren't working.

You're reading an idea over 20 years in the making! How does it feel?

When We Are Seeking

That awkward moment when someone in your life just mixes your insides up when you're trying to simply converse with them. It's simply biological at this point. You find the person so charming and practically perfect in every way and no matter how much you try to contain yourself, you just unravel at the seams.

But what if that's part of our charm? What if we're actually the cute and adorable ones because the person who is perceiving us is actually finding, what we deem as horrific, as absolutely perfect? And if that's the case, what would that look like?

We need to start accepting ourselves for who we are. Flaws and all. Love ourselves and watch everything else fall into place, even if it's not how we want it all to go.

Seek out the unknown when you accept yourself and know what you are seeking.

When I Met Benjamin Belmont Hastings

I hope I'm not the only one who used to do this and if so, I'm not sorry, but in college I imagined having a boyfriend and his name was Benjamin Belmont Hastings. Completely fabricated. It started off as a name to answer the question on who would be the perfect guy to date. I thought of a tall blonde who was classy. I have a weakness for blondes. I can't say no, what can I say? So, when I imagined how classy he'd be, I needed a name, and being the comic book fan that I was, my first instinct was to create a name that started with the same letter. There was a guy, Ben, I knew at the time who had a great smile and a ton of girlfriends. Not sure why I thought that might have been classy but I did like me some James Bond. Benjamin Belmont was born and the college I went to had a campus in Hastings, Michigan. Thus, Benjamin Belmont Hastings was born.

That's when my imagination started to spiral out of control with Benjamin. At first, it worked well. He was blonde. Have I mentioned that? Yes, he was definitely blonde, tall and classy. He had a great smile and liked all of the things that I liked.

So why didn't we spend time with each other? Besides the fact that he was completely made up, I decided to come up with a reason. So, I rewrote my biography on Benjamin Belmont Hastings.

That's when I started to add in my little quirks to the guy who no longer liked leaving his house. I like clean hands. I don't do well gardening as the dirt makes me feel, well, dirty. But I have to wash them the moment they are, so gardening is out of the question because gloves are suffocating. Quirks started blooming. As my biography started to bloom for Benjamin Belmont Hastings, I ended up showing my prose to my then English instructor, Elizabeth. She found Benjamin fascinating and introduced me to someone who dealt with Obsessive Compulsive Disorder, most commonly referred to as OCD. I found her absolutely amazing and we became quick friends. She was able to help me shape Benjamin Belmont Hastings out further until suddenly I had my story.

So, who is Benjamin Belmont Hastings?

He's my boyfriend.

When There Was Charlie

It's good to see you again, Charlie. I wrote about you in high school. Our views of the world were very similar. I didn't know who I was but I certainly knew what the world wanted me to be. After Spy Train, you are the second story I was going to put into my collection of shorts. I was proud of you. You were honest. You were unique. You were you and you weren't tied down to labels. I loved you.

So why did I put you away?

I was scared, Charlie. I was scared to write you and accept you because I was scared to accept myself. I was too busy explaining to the other students why I wasn't gay because if I admitted it, they'd hurt me more. I truly believed at the time they would have killed me. I heard it in the news. I saw it in shows. My own family talked so badly about our community, Charlie, that even though I loved you and I wanted to be me, I believed we were going to hell.

That's all that I knew, Charlie. I didn't know any better or have anyone else in my life to tell me otherwise. So, I tucked you away, Charlie. I hid you for a long time.

If it makes you feel any better, I did the same thing to myself.

I'm so sorry. You deserved better. We both did, didn't we?

So, Charlie, I'm letting you go. I'm taking you out of our hiding spot and I'm proudly displaying you for everyone to read. You're out. You've got this. I'm so proud of you. You were far braver than I was in high school. I hope you know that.

Now. Turn left, Charlie, turn left.

When There Was Sam

Be brave. Be you. Don't be afraid to take chances. And don't be afraid of loss, heart ache, disappointment or frustration. It's all part of being you.

Be kind to yourself. Don't be unforgiving to your mistakes. Don't shy away from life's disappointments because it makes the success all the sweeter.

Be courageous. Don't stay when you should walk away. Don't take on more than you can handle and make them take no for an answer. Take what you need and leave the rest behind.

Be honest. Be you. Don't be ashamed of the pieces of the puzzle that complete who you are. Don't hesitate to speak your truth and place that truth in a place of love, joy and peace.

Be. Be that person who walks up to someone in need, in solidarity, in acceptance, in love and hold out a hand in bravery, in kindness, in courage and in truth and say, "Hi. I am…"

When The Paper Was Black

I love legends. Lore. Tales of warning. I love the unseen horrors in movies because my imagination scares me more than what I could ever see in front of me. It's why stories like The Exorcist, Blair Witch, The Conjuring and to some extent Friday the 13th and Halloween have the capability of scaring me because what I don't see, or see where it's going to come from, that fills me with dread. It also excites me. I also find it fascinating that what can scare me doesn't necessarily scare others and vice versa.

I wanted to write a story where the readers didn't actually get to see the terror that lurks in the shadows of fear. In Apartment 1B, I touched on this similar theme. I wanted each reader who read Black Paper to imagine something different that was stalking the boy who dared to read its book. I also wanted the reader to doubt if it really exists or if the boy's own imagination was creating his own fear. The reader imagines the terror but is the boy imagining it too?

What actually exists on paper when it's black?

When Geneva Got Sick

For one of my studies in Children's Literature, I chose dark fables and fairy tales. I read a lot of Aesop and Grimm. I loved the dark undertone of the messages and yet somehow came out with a positive moral. Even Mother Goose's rhymes had some pretty dark themes. I mean if Peter, the pumpkin eater, put his wife in a pumpkin, then we all know what Peter did, right? And those glass slippers on Cinderella were torture! And if a fable has a fox and a wolf in it, you know things are about to get gruesome.

I tried my hand at a tale to mimic some common themes and elements and put them into my own dark tale. What I like about this tale is the deeper story this touches base on. Geneva had an illness that seemingly could not be cured and by the end of the story, it started to spread to the rest of the family or at least the fear of it spreading tempted the rest of them to drink the tea. We have a mother who was the main caregiver to Geneva and her mental health slowly started to unravel. For whatever reason, the husband overlooked the wife, or at least that is how she perceived it. Communication fell apart. Needs weren't being met and in her desire to be noticed, whether she truly had evil intentions or not, the wife sought out the local witch for help.

And like most witches, she seemed to have her own agenda. I love writing witches, I'll be honest.

I feel for this family. The wife needed to be looked after better and mental health needed to be addressed. Grief took hold of this family and shut it completely down.

And forgive me for saying, but they really made a goose out of their family.

I'll see myself out.

When I Drank Milk With My Coffee

Mike VS. The World.

Yes, it's true. I made an absolute fool out of myself. I truly am sorry. I just wanted to stand up for the woman feeding her infant in public. I didn't like seeing her being harassed by the older woman. I put my foot in it. Numerous times. Said all the wrong things. All good intentions aside, I turned to a babbling idiot, though in my defence, they did unite in the end. So, I accomplished my mission, I suppose?

I'll leave it with you.

When There Was A Hedge

Behind the Hedge is the most recent short story I've written and its sole purpose was to give a sort of conclusion to Charlie and Sam. I felt they deserved one but I wanted it open enough for the readers to decide the ending.

Sam's gender is not revealed. It's not supposed to be because I want the reader to either assign one or don't. Charlie's gender has a pronoun, however, it's still left up to the reader as to what that pronoun actually means.

Both stories are a sort of choose your own adventure and hopefully by the end of each one, you want Charlie to turn left and you want Sam to just reach out and speak. Behind the Hedge gives the readers that opportunity but it also leaves what happens next in the reader's hands.

What do they become afterwards?

I don't know. You tell me.

When I Was Reading The Books

I worked for Kellogg Community College Library. I loved the job and I was good at it. My supervisor, Rosie, however, did not think I did a good job. She kept catching me reading books or magazines as I was putting them away. She didn't seem to notice that I still got her jobs done that she assigned to me. In fact, I ended up starting to do more than what was required. I just couldn't seem to follow her explicit instruction. I was a rebel.

Every day for two weeks, I heard her say to me, "Don't read the books."

Finally, she had enough and fired me. The next time I went to the library I saw a girl working the counter. I will admit I felt a pinch of jealousy. I really did like the job. It's just that Rosie didn't like me.

I walked up to the girl, who was reading a magazine, and said, "Don't read the books."

We shared this knowing look. I never saw the same person working there for more than a few weeks and that's the only time I ever met a librarian that didn't want me to read.

When Assignments Show Talent

We all know the type. Chad. They're an absolute jerk and they know it. It's this toxicity that exists in some people and I can't help but wonder what holds them back from not only admitting that they're a big jerk but also following through the changes they need to make to undo it.

I also love Sal, who by just giving her name, reveals so much about this character. A common theme I have throughout Shorts is the idea that the readers are responsible for any labels they put on my characters. I'll give the clues or I won't. I'll avoid the details because it's the readers desire to put them in or don't.

Either way the voices are loud and clear and this story and Talent truly speak volumes.

When The Smoke Made A Trail

I love twisted tales. I've said this before and this is a perfect showcase.

I want to take note to the scene switch though. Here we have a mystery with three friends and their interaction shows a lot about their character and what their lives were like before the trail of smoke. But what I love, and I hope you loved too, was when the big reveal happens, we switch over very casually to a couple that discover the gruesome scene.

I also love the moment the couple take a moment to appreciate each other and say it almost simultaneously.

One last thing and it's a bit of a lecture, but it's an important one. Life is short. Fleeting. Blink of an eye things change. That text? That phone call? It can wait for the car to come to a complete stop.

When A Prince Wanted To Be A Princess

I was teaching the third grade and this class was having trouble getting along with each other. My first week was just watching them yell at each other and make fun of each other. They were not getting along. Fingers were being pointed in all directions. Even upwards. I had to take time to teach them a new way of communicating. I needed them to see the world differently than how they were seeing it.

My classroom became a team building exercise. Every single day. It was no longer about their own individual education. It was about our education. Together. And if we were going to make it through a successful year, we would have to do it together.

They were used to individual seats. Doing their individual things. I put them into groups. They named their tables. They were responsible for a little green cup that sat in the centre of the table for all members to reach. Points were given for kind words. At first, a simple thank you got a point. Or a please. They overused the words because it got them a free point.

Then I made it harder. The positive language was not expected. They had to work together. They had to treat each other with kindness. And when they were displeased with one another, they had to stop blaming each other for the mistakes. In fact, they had to start focusing on what other people were doing well and complimenting them on it. Then the points would come. I'd take the points away if they were negative, mean or blatantly screamed at each other.

But they still had issues accepting people who were different. Too different. Too unique. Anything that questioned what they understood in their world. And so, I told them a story.

"This is about a prince who wanted to be a princess," I started and the class freaked out. Most of them laughed. Some of them made faces and already made fun of the prince. Not one of those students sympathised with the prince at all. Because in their world a prince could only be a prince.

I began telling the story, the same one you read, to the students. They laughed at all the bits where the prince wanted to wear a dress. They actually liked Sir Easton. They agreed with him.

I told the story in different parts, too. When I brought up that it was story time, they'd either roll their eyes or laugh thinking it was a joke. Things started to change one day, though, when a student (a boy) raised his hand and asked, "Did the prince like to play with girl toys?"

I paused for a moment, "That's a good question. What do you guys think?"

And for a moment, we started talking about toys. They talked about what made a toy for girls and what made a toy for boys. An argument started to form because some of the girls said they played with those toys and some the boys argued that they played with some of the girl's toys. I sat back. I trusted them in their argument. I knew they'd watch what they say because they didn't want to lose points. They complimented each other on their ideas, even if they didn't agree. Sometimes they got a point. Sometimes they didn't. We were at a stage now where they no longer expected points but thanked me if I decided to give them one, which always ended up them getting an extra one.

When I continued the story, I noticed not so many of the students laughed as much anymore. They just accepted that the prince wanted to be a princess. Besides, if everyone could play with each other's toys, why couldn't they share clothes?

"My baby brother wears some of my old clothes," a girl shared with the class and this led to a long conversation about sharing clothes.

One boy even called out and said, "I try walking in my mom's shoes."

"So do I!" another boy exclaimed, "It's so hard to walk in them!"

And we discussed wearing parent's clothing for a while and I probably learnt about things their parents probably didn't want me to know.

Soon, Sir Easton became the bad guy. I didn't change the way I spoke or acted as him. He was exactly the same. I even started the story over one day at the request of the students. They were beginning to see the prince differently.

Then I got to the Knight In Shining Armour. I described the Knight's adventures in trying to save the prince. There was a moment in my story where the Knight kisses the hand of the prince.

"Ew, Mr. Stoneburner," one of the boys said, "That's so gross."

"Oh?" I stopped my story and looked down at him, "Why's that?"

"He's kissing a boy's hand!"

"Maybe the prince also wants to be a girl?" one of the girls asked.

"Why would a boy want to be a girl? They're gross," a boy added and I slowly started to make my way to his table suddenly. He changed his tune quickly, "Sorry. Sorry. Girls aren't gross. I just don't want to be a girl. No boy does."

Another boy spoke up, "Do you want to be a princess?"

"No!" the boy responded back.

"So, you're different and that's okay," one of the girls added. I added a point to her table and another one because she thanked me.

"Maybe the Knight is a girl," one of my meeker students suddenly said and I smiled.

"That's a good point," I added, "I actually haven't told you whether it's a boy or a girl."

I let the class discuss whether knights could be girls before we ended story time. By the time I had reached the end of the story that week, they no longer questioned the story. They accepted it and clapped their hands loudly when the Knight In Shining Armour danced with the Princess of Delovia. For the rest of the year, I enjoyed hearing stories from the girls pretending they were knights. Though none of the boys talked about becoming princesses, they didn't shy away from playing female characters during drama.

"It's okay, Mr. Stoneburner," a boy said, "I can play Mama Bear. I can even bring my mom's nightgown and slippers if you want."

No one laughed at him. Pointed fingers. Shouted. They

thought it was a great idea. They worked together. For years to come, even now, I'll come across those Year 3 students and they remember that year fondly.

"You taught us to accept each other just like the Princess of Delovia," the meeker student had said to me at their high school graduation.

But, that story was shelved. The school had heard what type of story I had been telling the students. Parents weren't happy. Behind closed doors I was lectured and was banned from telling that story or anything similar again.

So here it is. Out of hiding for the world to read in all its parts. No shame. Voices loud and clear.

Be a prince. Be a princess. Be both. Be a knight in shining armour. Be like those students at the end of the year who walked out my door loving each other for who they were not for who they thought they should be.

When We Need To Just Be

I never got to raise my voice like I wanted to as a child. I never got to in high school. A little bit in college but college ended and I was silenced once again. Harder. Harsher.

We all have our own little red shorts to wear. Every single one of us. But not everyone gets to hang those red shorts out for everyone to see. This story, and the stories that came before it, share one common theme. Appreciate each other. Appreciate yourself. Don't strive to be something you're not. Don't be that person who knows they're awful. Be that person who knows that they're great.

Turn left and let others turn with you. Speak up when you know you should. Stop worrying all the time that who you are is anything less than the sum of your parts. Be the person that you add up to be, accept it and love it for what it is. Flaws and all.

Just be!

And for the love of all things, read the books. Read them.

Even if it gets you fired.

Books by the Author

In-Rel Trilogy
Book 1 - Silver
Book 2 - Coming Soon

He Was a Boy Who Smiled
Book 1 - Phoenix Rising
Book 2 - Phoenix Falling

Shorts
A collection of short stories

We Need To Talk About This
Hanging On The Wall
Inclusive Love
Silenced Violence

Novella
Apartment 1B

About Michael

Michael Stoneburner lives in Sydney, Australia with their husband Joel. Michael was a primary teacher for almost 10 years before focusing all of their time on their writing. They donated their time to the local writing groups where they helped organise publications, radio shows and public readings.

He Was A Boy Who Smiled Book One and Book Two are now available. Book Three is on its way! They also wrote a series of short stories called Shorts that bring inclusive characters from the LGBT+ community, something they wished they had more growing up.

Michael enjoys observing humanity and interactions and it shows in Apartment 1B. Michael recharges their psyche with poetry and has released a collection of poetry. They also released Book One of their In-Rel fantasy series, Silver.

Michael is an advocate for mental health, working as a Peer Support person and has worked extensively with survivors of Domestic Violence, Inequality and Mental Illness. Each of these topics are addressed in their poetry anthologies. Michael continues to work on their website where they released free to read poetry, fan fiction, guest bloggers and personal thoughts and self-reflection.

Visit michaelstoneburner.com for more.